BRAWLER'S WEAKNESS

TENNESSEE THUNDERBOLTS

GINA AZZI

THREE CITIES PUBLISHING LLC

ONE

MAISY

"YOU ARE A STRONG AND CONFIDENT WOMAN," I tell my reflection. My blonde hair has been carefully curled, casual beach waves that dust the tops of my shoulders.

I lean closer to the mirror to apply mascara.

"Today is the first day of the rest of your life," I remind myself, capping the mascara wand.

"Good things are on the horizon. You just have to be open and willing to accept them." I take a deep inhale, slowly let the breath out, and grin when the timer on my oven dings.

"And making a great first impression includes sweet treats." I finish my moment of manifesting and hurry into the kitchen to remove the muffins before they burn.

Ooh, but they are perfect! I beam as I stare at my baking creation. It's one of my grandmother's swear-by recipes, and the first one Mom taught me when I was five. Back when she still enjoyed baking with me. Before the butter and sugar became a no-go for my diet and muffins too fattening for breakfast. I inhale the delicious aroma filling my kitchen.

Fluffy muffins with big blueberries that look gooey and delicious and smell like a bakery.

I carefully plate the muffins and wrap them in tinfoil, set on taking them into the office for my first day of work at my new job.

Starting in Human Resources with the Tennessee Thunderbolts hockey team is a far cry from my former position as attorney-at-law Tim Clancy's personal assistant. But already, it feels better.

I'm done with Tim and his constant belittling of my intelligence and comments about my weight. I'm a strong and confident woman who bakes a mean muffin and is an organizing whiz.

Sure, nerves are ping-ponging around my stomach and my hands are clammy. But I'm stuffing my anxiety back where it belongs and embracing the day. *Today*. Good things are on the horizon.

When the muffins and my purse are stashed by the door, I make one last trip into the bathroom. My sundress, a pale blue, has a tie at the waist to punch it up. I've paired it with a soft white cardigan, pearl earrings, and espadrilles. I'm flirting the line of professional and casual, just like my best friend, Mila Lewis, the team's personal trainer, recommended.

After nearly a decade of pencil skirts and blazers, it's refreshing to wear something pretty and fun to work. It's another sign that my life is improving.

"Strong and confident." I meet my reflection with a steely gaze before winking at myself.

Then, I swipe up my purse and muffins and drive to The Honeycomb, the team's arena and my new office.

As Adele's voice softly fills my speakers, I stop at a red light. My phone chirps with a new message and I glance at my purse, wondering if it's my parents, my sister Missy, Mila, or my boyfriend Josh messaging to wish me luck on my first day.

The light turns green, and I sing one song, loud and off-key, before pulling into the parking lot. I settle my purse across my chest, carefully lift the tray with muffins, and with my head held high, enter The Honeycomb and its fulfilling promise of change.

My phone beeps again and I stall. What if something's wrong? What if Missy needs me? Or Mila forgot to tell me something important, something pertaining to the Thunderbolts, before I start my first day?

Sighing, I pull my phone out of my purse, pulling up short as the words on the screen register in my mind.

Josh: I can't do this anymore. I'm done.

What the fuck?

Josh: I'll get my shit out of your place by the end of today.

A bubble of disbelief swells in my throat. Shaking my head, I clutch my phone and resume walking toward the main office.

Josh is...breaking up with me? *Via text.*

It's so ridiculous, so hurtful and humiliating and a cruel twist to the past year of our relationship that my shoulders shake. My lips rub together. My hands tremble. And I laugh.

We weren't relationship goals or anything, but I thought he'd at least have the decency to dump me in person. The last few months, we've been less like a couple and more like roommates anyway. I can't say I'm surprised at the demise of our relationship but shit, a damn text?

You know, it's just like Josh to take the easy way out. To solve his problems behind a screen, behind a distraction. He's such a coward and—

"Ooh!" I shriek as I collide with a moving body. The muffin tray flips up, all eighteen muffins hitting me square in the chest, the aluminum foil drifting to the floor like a paper airplane.

"Watch where the fuck you're going!" an angry voice shouts.

I stumble back a step, nearly tripping over my feet, at the harsh tone, the angry, wild eyes.

The guy, one of the players but I don't know who, grips the back of his neck, a quick look of remorse flaring in his eyes. "Fuck!" he swears again, sidestepping me.

Shocked and uncertain, I glance around the quiet front office. The silence is too loud, with too many eyes staring at me in varying degrees of surprise, horror, or embarrassment. *For me.*

I screw my eyes shut for a heartbeat and let the mortification, the pure *cringe*, wash over me.

You are strong and confident. You will not cry. You're...fine.

I force my eyes open, and they snag on the receptionist/office manager, Betty, who made me feel welcomed during my interview for the job. She opens her mouth and—

"You okay?" A gruff voice, followed by a gentle touch to my elbow.

I look up and gasp, this time for an entirely different reason.

Axel Daire peers down at me, his dark eyes midnight, an angry slash twisting his lips. But his touch is gentle. His eyes are filled with so much concern—*for me*—that tears prick the backs of my eyes.

"Maisy." He says my name, his tone raw, as if he understands the depths of my humiliation. As if he can taste the mortification currently turning my cheeks red.

I glance down at my dress, my chest covered in muffin, my cardigan smeared in blueberry.

Don't cry. You're strong and confident. Don't cry. Good things are—

"Betty, she'll be back tomorrow," Axel announces, his tone sharp.

"Of course," Betty agrees, rushing over and gently turning me back toward the door. She stuffs a handful of napkins into my clenched fingers and lowers her voice. "You get cleaned up and tomorrow, we'll start over. Don't worry, the first week is onboarding. Lots of paperwork and nothing you're missing out on." She chuckles and I know I should at least smile or say thank you or react. Instead, I stare at Betty and Axel in a daze.

My phone chirps again and I close my eyes, remembering Josh's message. He's probably at our place, *my place*, right now, packing away pieces of a home I wanted too much to believe in.

My heart aches. A damn text message. Is that all I'm worth? Is that the sum of value Josh views the last year of my life?

"Come on, Mais," Axel's tone is soft, at odds with the fierce lines of his expression. He wraps an arm around my shoulders and steers me out of The Honeycomb.

Numbly, I follow along, not putting up a protest as he tucks me into the passenger seat of his truck and pulls the seat belt across my chest, buckling me in.

It's not until he turns on his truck and music fills the space between us that I snap out of it.

"My car—" I point to my small VW Bug.

"You shouldn't drive when you're upset." He puts the gearstick in drive and pulls out of the parking lot.

I turn to look at him, surprised but oddly comforted, that he's here. Helping me. Taking care of me.

Axel Daire is a giant of a man. When he enters a room, he commands the energy in it. He eats up space and expands with it. Not with loud words or flashy clothing, but with his steadfast silence, his quiet observation.

Axel Daire is a man who perceives things without your having to say them. He's gruff and growly. He rarely smiles and hardly laughs. But when he looks at me, he sees straight to my soul, and the compassion in his gaze almost breaks me. It's the same as the first night I met him. Over the summer, in a crowded sports bar. Mila was introducing me to Devon, one of the players and now, her boyfriend. But that night, it was Axel who held my gaze, who bought me a drink, who offered me a ride home. It was Axel who *saw* me.

He heads in the direction of my house, having dropped me off a time or two after a night out with Mila and Devon.

Still, it surprises me that he remembers where I live and drives there quietly, unbothered by the silence, the elephant, in the space between us.

I glance down and note that my hands are trembling.

"River never should have spoken to you like that," Axel says after a beat, his eyes drifting toward me for a blink. "He'll apologize," he adds with a finality that I don't question. Because if need be, Axel, also known as Brawler, will make River apologize.

"It's fine," I say, my voice sounding small.

"No, it's not," Axel's tone is hard.

I sigh. "It's not just that. I, my, Josh broke up with me."

Axel's neck snaps in my direction, his jaw locked, his eyes flaring. "What?"

I lick my lips. "My boyfriend, well, ex-boyfriend, Josh,

broke up with me *via text message*. I received the message right as River ran into me. It wasn't his fault, I was standing in the middle of the hallway, staring at my phone. I wasn't paying attention."

"He didn't even check that you're okay," Axel bites out. I frown, trying to understand his words, until I realize he's still talking about River. Patton! River's last name flies into my head. He plays right wing. But then, Axel adds, "What a douche. A text message?"

I snort, nodding. "Awful, isn't it?"

Axel shrugs, turning on his blinker to make a right-hand turn. "It's his fucking loss, Maisy."

"Yeah," I agree. "The fact that he dumped me through a text is proof enough that I dodged a bullet."

Axel glances at me, as if to mark the sincerity of my words. Satisfied, he turns back to the road and nods. "Exactly."

But when we turn onto my street and I note Josh's truck in the driveway, my heart drops to the floor and I feel like vomiting.

Scenarios from the past few months drift through my mind. Josh blowing off Sunday dinner with my family because he had to work but instead, went to his buddy Steve's place to play video games. The way he took his phone with him, even to the bathroom, as if he didn't want me to look at it even though I never snooped. Or how we haven't had sex in months and when I tried to initiate, he'd make an offhanded comment about my body. As if I repulsed him. As if he couldn't stand to see me naked. Tears prick the corners of my eyes at my own weakness.

I know I deserve more than what Josh gave me. I know I'm worthy of a better, more committed partner. I know all this and still, the thought of walking into my house and confronting him makes me feel like I'm breaking out in hives. My skin prickles, my heart rate increases, and my breathing doubles.

"I can't go in there," I nearly wheeze.

Axel idles next to the curb in front of my place, his eyes on mine. "I can go with you if—"

"No." I shake my head. "Please. I don't want to confront Josh. I just want, I want to get out of here." My eyes are pleading and after a long, searching look, Axel nods.

He scans my body, his eyes lingering on the blueberry smudges. I'm hot mess express right now. The sensible thing would be to go into *my house*, change my clothes, and leave. But that would mean confronting Josh. I shiver at the thought, hating any type of confrontation. And maybe even worse than exchanging words with Josh, would be Axel witnessing it.

"Do you trust me?" His voice is so low, I think I misunderstood.

My eyebrows dip as I stare at him.

He tilts his head to the side. "Do you trust me, Maisy?"

"Yes," I breathe out, realizing that I do. I trust Axel Daire more than most men, even though I hardly know him. He gives off that vibe, always checking that his teammates have a ride home at the end of a night out. Always inserting himself into the middle of a team quarrel or the showdowns that have taken place between the Bolts and the Knoxville Coyotes football team at the sports bar, Corks. Hell, he even excuses himself to check in with his daughter, a student at the University of Tennessee.

Maybe it's because he's a dad. Maybe it's because he's lived through shit, raising a daughter from a very young age. Or maybe, it's because he's truly one of those unicorn men. Caring, considerate, and compassionate. Whatever the reason, I don't question him as he pulls away from the curb and turns back onto Main Street.

Instead, I settle back into the car seat, clutch the seat belt where it cuts between my breasts, and stare out the window.

When we pull up in front of a boutique I love, my gaze swings to Axel. How does he even know about this place? My eyes widen, conveying my thoughts.

The strangest thing happens. One side of his mouth tugs upward, curling into an almost-smile that smooths out his roughness. God, he's gorgeous. Strong, fierce, and *beautiful.*

"I got you, okay?" His voice is so gentle, I feel like crying again.

Luckily, I don't. I watch as Axel slips out of the truck and enters the boutique.

It's a beautiful shop, filled with stylish summer dresses, eclectic accessories, and must-have cowgirl boots. It effortlessly blends boho and chic and western styles and is a staple store for the University of Tennessee sorority girls as well as young professional women.

In fact, there's a dress in the window I've been admiring for weeks, but the V-neck is deep and I'm always worried about it being *too* much. Will it look like I'm trying *too* hard?

My whole life, I've been *too* much but never in the right ways. Only in the ways that men, or my mother, have commented on. Too thick, too big, too slow. But when Axel looks at me, it feels like he doesn't see any of my natural shortcomings. Instead, he sees me and it's right.

I turn away from the window, controlling my emotions before he comes back. This morning, I set out with the intention of turning over a new leaf, of embracing a new beginning. I never thought that would lead to sitting in the passenger seat of Axel Daire's F-150, but I'm not mad about it.

I am strong and confident. And as Axel steps out of the boutique, his shoulders filling up the doorway, his hair pulled away from his face and tied in a messy bun at the back of his head, I realize it's still true. Good things are on the horizon.

He slides back behind the wheel, wordlessly handing me a shopping bag. My stomach twists with a flicker of panic. Did he buy the correct size? Or did he size down, the way Josh always did? Even though Josh knew my dress size, he'd always choose a size smaller and give me a look like, "you could lose weight if you tried," when it didn't zip fully or the buttons pulled.

I let out a nervous exhale and reach into the bag, my heart in my throat when I see *the* dress. The soft peach fabric, decorated with a thousand tiny wildflowers. The one with the deep V neckline. I take a sly glance at the tag and want to weep in relief when I note the size. My size.

Axel's watching me carefully.

I clear my throat, my emotions clogging my ability to speak. "Thank you, Axel." I dig into my purse, pulling out my wallet to grab some cash.

Axel's hand darts out, settles over mine, and stops my movements. He shakes his head, his eyes on my wallet. "You're welcome." It's all he says before pulling away from the boutique and pointing his truck in a new direction.

I let out a shaky breath and settle back against the seat, clutching the dress in my hands. He bought me a dress. A beautiful, correctly sized, dress.

Right now, I don't need to know where we're going. Or

why. I feel so much better just being here, next to Axel, feeling *seen*. And cared for.

Still... "I should go back to work."

"Betty said to come in tomorrow."

"What about you? Don't you have to go back? You can drop me at Mila's." Since my best friend's parents passed away a few years ago, I've had a key to her place.

Axel slides his hand over the top of the steering wheel and shoots me a quick glance. "Nah. I had an early skate and hit the weight room already. I'm free for the rest of the day."

"Oh."

"Are you hungry?"

"What?"

He almost smiles. Again. "Are you hungry?" His eyes slip down to my chest for a moment. "Because I've been starving since I realized I've missed out on trying one of your famous muffins."

I think it's the most words I've ever heard him say in a single stretch. "I'll bake you more." I blush. "As a thank you." I hold up the dress.

"Come eat with me and we'll call it even."

"Okay," I agree softly. Stunned.

Did the universe send Axel to me today? Is the cosmos playing a joke? Is this, right now, the new beginning I didn't see coming?

He tips his chin down and turns the music up slightly. We ride the rest of the way in silence, but it's comfortable. Things between Axel and me hold an easiness that I never experienced off the bat with other men. I don't feel like he's judging me. Or criticizing. Instead, it feels like he truly wants to be here, in this moment, with me.

The thought makes me smile and I turn to look out the window so he won't think I'm losing it.

When he parks in the lot for a trendy cafe near campus, I quirk an eyebrow. "You know all the cool spots."

He ducks his head. "Lola."

"Ah, that makes sense." I open the door and slide from the truck. Of course his university student daughter would keep him in the know. It's probably how he knew of the boutique too.

Axel's hand hovers over the small of my back as we step into the cafe. He's not touching me and yet, I feel the heat of his large palm. I sense the protectiveness in his stance, and I shuffle back a half step, wanting to feel his touch. Wanting to be rooted in the kindness he's showing me.

Once we're seated, I hold up the shopping bag with my new dress. "I'll be right back."

"Take your time."

I scurry toward the restroom. As soon as the door is locked behind me, I glance at my reflection and blanche.

Blueberry stains my cardigan and dress. Bits of muffin still stick to the swells of my breasts. My hair is a mess, the soft waves of the morning giving way to erratic curls.

I take a deep breath. "You're confident," I scold my reflection.

Then, I clean off the muffin bits with some water and paper towel. I take off my clothes and pull on the new dress, loving the feel of the material as it slides down my body. I fix the bodice and my eyebrows shoot up at how incredible my chest looks. The material clings to my breasts, making them appear high and perky. It skims along my waist and over my hips, in a flattering A-line, that is feminine. Flirty.

I give a little laugh and twirl.

It's not my usual look, but I love it. I feel pretty and *confident*.

On a day that has gone sideways, I have Axel Daire to thank for reminding me that that's who I am. For showing me that my manifesting has come true.

Good things are on the horizon.

TWO
AXEL

MY PALM IS TOO large for the dainty coffee mug. I'm holding it so tightly, my knuckles creak and I feel the clay nearly give way. Shit. I relax my grip and drag my eyes away from the corridor that leads to the restrooms.

Maisy Stratford is fine. Sure, she was shaken up. And yeah, River Patton better fucking apologize for barreling into her and ruining her dress. Not to mention her day. Don't get me started on her pathetic excuse for an ex-boyfriend. I've never met Josh but everything I've heard about him tells me all I need to know. Someone should have knocked him out back in middle school and set the entitled prick in his place.

I heave out a sigh, but it doesn't quell the protective edge slicing through my veins, mixing with adrenaline.

Maisy Stratford is fine. She handled everything—the muffin fiasco, her breakup, my choosing her a dress—with more grace than most women I know.

A dreadful thought runs through my mind and my eyes cut back to the corridor. What if she's in the bathroom right now, crying her eyes out? What if she managed to hold it together until we arrived here, and now, she's unraveling, alone?

I have a twenty-one-year-old daughter; I understand the complex, not to mention spectacular, emotional range of women.

I work a swallow, about to stand and stride toward the corridor, when Maisy turns the corner and my heart clogs my throat, my chest caving inward like a hit.

Maisy Stratford is fucking gorgeous.

Blonde waves that dance across the tops of her shoulders, blue eyes the color of the Caribbean at daybreak, and curves—delicious, natural, real curves—I want to sink my fingers into. The dress hugs them all, and as she skims her hands over her hips, a small smile flits across her face.

That smile makes me feel like I won the fucking lottery. Twice.

She likes the dress. She trusted me and I delivered the thing, the feeling, she was searching for. I made her smile when her day is falling apart.

I lean back in my seat, slowly releasing a breath to get a grip. My heart is beating too fast, my knee bounces under the table, nervous. Hell, even my beard feels itchy, like I'm a punk-ass kid posing as a grown man. With Maisy, I feel like a rookie, about to take the ice for my first big game, instead of a seasoned player whose been around a time or two.

Maisy walks over to the table, and I can't stop staring at her. When she arrives at the table side, she nervously nibbles the corner of her mouth.

"Thanks again for the dress." She pulls out the chair across from mine and sits down.

I clear my throat, feeling the tips of my ears burn, which

is ridiculous. "You look"—Maisy looks up and I freeze. *Beautiful. Gorgeous. Perfect*—"nice."

She smiles. "Thanks, Axel."

I nod and bury my head in the menu. Nice? That was my best adjective? Why can't I act normal around Maisy? Why can't I be more like my affable, charming brother, Asher? If he was here, he'd know exactly what to say. He wouldn't be faltering, hiding behind a menu, like me.

From the first time I met Maisy, when Mila dragged her to drinks with some guys on the team, I couldn't tear my eyes away. But that was when she was dating Josh and I knew all I could be was a casual acquaintance, a guy to order her a drink and make sure she had a ride home.

But now, she's single. And that opened a door of possibilities I've never let myself consider. Because I don't date or have serious relationships. I have Lola; I'm a dad. A girl dad. That's always come first, before everything.

My last real relationship, when Lola was eight, went sideways after two years and the devastation Lola felt at the loss of my ex-girlfriend in her life was enough for me to pump the breaks.

Marisol moved on quickly, finding the commitment she said I couldn't give her, only one year later. She was married, a homeowner, and a mother all in the span of two years. Lola sobbed when the Christmas card showing off Marisol's beautiful baby girl arrived. And I'd be lying if I said it didn't feel like getting stabbed in the chest.

But Lola's grown now...

"I love it here." Maisy breaks the silence, glancing around the eclectic cafe, with Andy Warhol prints on the walls, hanging greenery, and mismatched coffee mugs.

"Me too," I admit. "Lola and I come here for brunch every Sunday."

Maisy's eyes light up at the mention of Lola, which surprises me because most women are either shocked or disappointed when they learn I have a daughter. I mean, Maisy already knew I was a dad, but we haven't talked about Lola much.

"That's a nice tradition. My dad and I used to do monthly dinner dates when I was a student at UT. The first Wednesday of the month," she laughs, recalling a memory. "We almost always had breakfast for dinner at Betsy's Diner."

"You were a Volunteer?" I didn't know she went to the University of Tennessee, like Lola.

"Good ol' Rocky Top."

I grin, nodding at the reference to the university and its football program. "So, you're a football fan."

Maisy wrinkles her nose, as if she doesn't want to admit it to me.

I huff out a breath that sounds like a chuckle.

"I was raised on *Friday Night Lights* and tailgates," she explains, shrugging innocently.

"It seems that way around here." I look around the cafe but I mean the entire state of Tennessee. It's no secret that the Knoxville Coyotes, the Pride of Southern Football, hold the love and respect of the state while the Thunderbolts, and hockey in general, are newcomers. We don't have a fraction of the fan base or support as football.

"I'm looking forward to the hockey season," she says, her eyes sincere. "I haven't followed hockey before, but it seems like a good year to learn."

"Because you're now a Bolt and Mila is the team trainer?"

She shrugs, confirming my suspicion.

"If you have any questions about the game, you know who to ask." I lean closer over the table.

Maisy bites the corner of her mouth again and holy shit, am I flirting? Is she? Are we...feeling each other out?

"Hey there, Daire," a pointed voice announces.

I turn to look at the server and nearly do a double take as I come face to face with Jasmine Cates, Lola's best friend and roommate.

"Jas, what are you doing here?" I ask.

She arches an eyebrow, silently calling me out. Together, Lola and Jas have been on a mission to set me up with women ranging from the Mother Hen at their sorority house to the librarian to the woman who runs the boutique in town where I bought Maisy's dress. The appreciative glint in Jasmine's eye as she takes in Maisy lets me know the dress isn't lost on her.

Jas holds up a small notebook and pencil. "I got a job."

"Seriously?" I cough, trying not to laugh.

She rolls her eyes. "Yes, D, seriously." She shortens my surname, Daire, to her causal D. She wrinkles her nose as if it pains her to admit it and I immediately feel bad. And concerned.

Jasmine is my daughter's best friend and over the past few years, she's become my surrogate kid too. She often joins Lol and me for Sunday breakfast. She's a regular at my house to do her laundry. And when Lola drank too much at her first party freshman year and couldn't stop vomiting, Jasmine knew enough to call me for help, to walk her through it, to monitor Lola's behavior.

"Is everything okay?" I ask, sitting up straighter.

Across from me, I feel Maisy studying me.

Jas nods. "Yeah. All good."

"We'll talk Sunday."

She snorts, her eyes darting to Maisy. "Hell yeah, we will."

I blow out an exasperated breath. "Maisy, meet Lola's best friend and another pain in my ass, Jasmine Cates."

Maisy smiles. "Hi, Jasmine. It's nice to meet you."

"Same!" Jas smiles at Maisy, her eyes dancing. "I love your dress!"

"Oh!" Maisy blushes, glancing down at the peach material. "Thank you."

"Can I get you guys something to drink? Or eat? The Nutella French toast is bomb. So are the tostada rancheros if you're leaning vegan."

I grip the underside of the table. Jasmine is going to have a field day with this, and I know it won't be long, ten minutes max, until Lola is on my case too. They're going to want to know *everything*. Oh, Sunday breakfast will be long and painful.

"I'll stick with the classic breakfast, please," Maisy orders. "Scrambled for the eggs. And I'd love, desperately need, an oat latte."

"You got it." Jas scribbles down her order and begins to walk away.

"Hey, what about me?" I call after her.

She laughs. "I got you, D."

I shake my head. "Sorry."

"For what?" Maisy asks, amused.

I sigh. "Jasmine is going to call Lola in about ten seconds. And then both of them will be chirping in my ear." I don't mean to sound miserable but...I wish my daughter and her best friend would give my dating life a rest.

Rather than appear put off, Maisy laughs. And it's like music, soft and melodious. "Does Lola want you to date?"

"Desperately," I admit. "She says I'm now at an age

where I should seek happiness." I air quote around "seek happiness," using Lola's words, and Maisy laughs again. "I swear, I don't know what the hell she's talking about half the time."

"Things change that much from when you were growing up?" Her eyes hold a playful, teasing glint.

"Ha," I mock laugh and her smile grows. "It feels that way. I'm an old thirty-six," I admit.

Maisy's eyes soften. Hesitantly, she asks, "How old were you when you had Lola?"

I pause. I never share these details. In fact, I usually avoid bringing Lola up, so openly, with women I don't know well. But with Maisy, I want to talk about things that *matter*. And no one, nothing, matters more to me than my daughter. "Sixteen. Her mother, Anna, and I were high school sweethearts. We were way out of our depth, unprepared, when Anna learned she was pregnant."

"That must have been hard," Maisy says. Her expression is thoughtful, her tone compassionate. It's not pitying or judging the way most women react, and for that, I'm grateful enough to continue.

"Anna and I broke up when Maisy was about a year old. It wasn't bitter or dramatic or anything. We both knew we wanted more out of a romantic relationship, but we were friends, co-parents, and Lola was the glue that held us together. I was offered scholarships around the country for hockey and Anna agreed to move with Lola so I could still be involved in her life. After I got signed to the Rams, they came to Seattle with me. It was there that Anna met Ben, her now husband, and started a new family."

"Was that hard?"

I shake my head. "Not the way you'd think. I was happy, relieved even, that Anna found someone who loves her the way she deserves to be loved. And Lola gained another male role model. Anna and Ben have two boys who call me uncle and I'm glad Lola got to have siblings, brothers who drove her a little bit batty. She's close with them."

"That's...wow, that's really evolved of y'all." Maisy shakes her head, like she's having a hard time wrapping her mind around the functionality of it all. But it works. Anna and I committed to being parents and we always put Lola first.

I shrug. "It wasn't always easy, but I'm glad Anna is Lola's mother. She's always a mom first, always there for Lola, and we never had all that dramatic bullshit I've seen other guys on my teams go through in their marriages."

"So, you've never been married?"

"No."

Maisy nods, taking this information in. When Jas delivers her coffee and my orange juice, she shoots me a wink and I stifle a groan. The third degree is coming; I know it.

"Thanks, Jasmine." Maisy takes a sip of her coffee.

"What about you?" I ask, wanting to turn the attention away from myself. I hate talking about myself, my past, my life. With Maisy, I want to open up more, which is new for me. But I've said more to her than anyone in Tennessee, save for Lola and Jas, and I'm ready for her to take center stage.

"I've never been married," she laughs. "I don't know if I've ever even been in love." A line forms in between her eyebrows, as if she's pondering this, recalling a string of past relationships.

"Ever?" I find that hard as fuck to believe. Men must have fallen for Maisy Stratford. Either she's in denial or completely oblivious.

Maisy purses her lips and shakes her head.

"Even with the...the ex?"

"Definitely not with Josh." She answers so quickly, I wonder if she's telling the truth or nursing a bruised ego along with her heart. "At first, I thought so. But over the past few months...the signs were there."

"What signs?"

She gives me a small smile that doesn't reach her eyes. She's grasping for casual when it's obvious she's hurt. That protective edge sweeps through me again. "His moving in but never contributing toward the mortgage or groceries or anything. His changing jobs without talking to me about it, but trying to convince me to stay at Tim's law firm when he knew, he knew, how hard it was."

I gulp, my hands finding my orange juice glass and once again, squeezing too hard. I've seen firsthand how Tim spoke to Maisy when she was his assistant. He was awful, degrading. His treatment of Maisy is the main reason why I didn't retain him.

"And...other stuff," she lets out on a sigh. "Deep down, I know I'm better off without him. But the suddenness of the breakup, the text message"—a soulless chuckle—"it hurts, you know? Like, I'm not even worth a phone call?"

Slowly, I nod. Her pain is stamped across her face, written in the lines around her mouth, present in the gray ring at the edge of her irises.

I reach across the table and place my hand over hers, flattening it between the table and my palm. "You deserve better, Maisy. More." My voice is gruff, as if the words had to be scraped from the column of my throat.

But Maisy hears the thread of truth because she smiles. A real smile that lights her face and causes me to feel like the biggest, best man in the universe.

"Thank you for saying that, Axel."

I nod, removing my hand, as Jasmine appears with our orders.

Again, she's failing to hide her excitement at this new development in my personal life. Again, I ignore her. I keep my eyes trained on Maisy, wondering how I got so lucky.

Today, of all days, I was in the right place at the right time. For the right reason.

For a man who doesn't believe in chance, it sure does feel like kismet.

———

WHEN I PULL into Maisy's driveway, Josh's truck is gone. She breathes out a sigh of relief, ducking her head as she tucks a wave of hair behind her ear.

"Thanks again, Axel," Maisy says softly. "You really managed to turn things around for me today."

"It wasn't me."

"Sure, it was." She glances down at her dress. "And I love the dress."

One side of my mouth curls. "I'm glad."

She nods, her eyes holding mine for a moment that lasts longer than it should, but not long enough.

When I clear my throat, she jumps. "Right." She opens the passenger door. "See you around, then."

"See you tomorrow," I remind her, since there's no way I'm not passing by the main office every chance I get, especially knowing she'll be there. Every day. Nine to six.

She waves, her keys clutched in her hand, before unlocking her front door and disappearing inside.

I sit in her driveway, admiring the simple bungalow.

There are window boxes filled with flowers and the front door is yellow, like sunshine.

Her house looks like one of those starter homes a young couple would bring a baby home to. Even from the outside, it's cozy and inviting, warm. I move to pull out of the driveway when her purse, a practical navy blue, catches my eye. It's tucked between the center console and the seat, so Maisy must have forgotten it when it slipped.

I put the truck in park, grab her bag, and make my way to her front door. Curiosity washes over me at the prospect of seeing inside her home, at learning more about her. Is it just as inviting inside? Does it give off the same warmth as her smiles, the same sincerity as her eyes?

I knock on the door, surprised when it nudges open. The keyless entry numbers light up but no code has been set to relock the door.

I frown. Does she usually leave her door unlocked and cracked open?

Pushing inside, I call out, "Maisy?"

Nothing. No response, just static silence.

My concern skyrockets in under two seconds and I barrel into the house, wondering if something sinister has happened with Josh. I enter so quickly, I nearly knock Maisy over from behind.

"Fuck," I swear, wrapping my arms around her middle to keep us upright.

Maisy's body is still in my arms, frozen in shock.

"Maisy?" I turn her around, placing my hands on her shoulders and give her a little shake. "What is it? What's wrong?"

Her eyes meet mine, confused and...hurt. "He took the furniture."

What? I look over her shoulder and, "That motherfucker." Her living room is empty, save for the television mount still stuck to the wall. He even swiped her TV.

"He took my furniture," she whispers to herself, disbelief heavy in her tone.

Coldness tracks through my veins as I shut down the anger radiating from me like a fucking heat source. Maisy doesn't need my anger right now; she needs me to step up.

"Sit here." I guide her away from the empty living room and into the dining area, praying I find a table. I breathe a sigh of relief when we enter the kitchen instead. I help her onto one of the barstools at the kitchen island.

Moving around her kitchen like I've been here a hundred times instead of a hundred seconds, I fill a glass of water and place it in front of her.

Then, I pull out my phone and call Mila.

"Axe?" she answers, surprised.

"Get to Maisy's house now," I demand. "And bring Devon."

"Wait, what? What's wrong? Is she—"

"She's fine." My tone is clipped, my anger barely concealed. "Just come, okay?"

"Yeah, okay. Devon and I will be there in ten."

I hang up the phone, tossing it onto the countertop.

Maisy's expression is heartbreaking, her eyes helpless. She slumps in her seat, defeat heavy on her shoulders, and I want to put my fist through the goddamn wall.

I step beside her and wrap an arm around her shoulders, tentative, gentle. The way I would to Jasmine or one of Anna's boys.

But when Maisy turns into my embrace, all bets are off and I hug the shit out of her. I pull her into my arms and hold her close, murmuring soothing sounds and running my fingers through her hair.

I erase whatever space existed between us—polite, comfortable, casual acquaintanceship—and let her know that I'm here for her.

That I care about her.

And that I'm not fucking going anywhere.

THREE
MAISY

"WHAT'S GOING ON?" Mila asks before she's through the front door.

Axel stands back to make room for Devon who, like him, is a big, burly hockey player.

"Shit," Devon mutters when he takes in my tearstained cheeks and the backdrop of my empty living room.

"He took your TV?" Mila gasps, staring at the wall mount.

I nod, miserable. "When Axel tried to drop me off this morning—"

"This morning?" Mila questions, her eyes narrowing.

"There was a muffin incident," Axel says in a gruff voice.

Mila narrows her eyes at him, and Devon cocks his head, confused.

"Josh's truck in the driveway, and I didn't, I couldn't..." I search for words to explain my avoidance. Damn me and my dumb fear of confrontation. If I'd waltzed in, would I have discovered Josh pulling the TV off the wall?

"We decided to get a late breakfast instead," Axel fills in.

"Uh-huh," Devon says, shooting Axel a questioning look that Axel ignores. Hm, does Devon think there's something between Axel and me? Could there be something between us?

"And when you came back now, everything was gone?" Mila asks, sticking to the important part of the conversation.

"Yeah," Axel confirms.

"That snake!" Mila paces in front of the kitchen island, glaring at my empty living room. "I can't believe, well, no, I can believe that he would do something like this because he's just so, so—"

"Pathetic," I offer.

Mila growls.

"Where would he go?" Devon asks.

I drift around my living room, running my hands across the freshly painted walls I paid for just last month after Josh complained the taupe color was too depressing. Now, they're eggshell white and bare because along with the television, Josh took my framed vintage Champagne posters.

"Steve's," Mila and I say in unison, mentioning Josh's best friend.

"Unless..." I whisper, the thought too embarrassing to continue aloud. I try to swallow it back, but three heads swing in my direction.

"Unless what?" Mila's tone is gentle.

"Unless he met someone," I admit the secret kernel of unproven truth I carry around in my chest. Deep down, given Josh's behavior the last few months, given how depressingly long it's been since we've had sex, given all the late nights and sudden obsession with his cell phone, I'm pretty sure he met someone else. A skinnier, blonder, bouncier version of me.

At my confession, Axel's eyes blaze, the ire in their depths so strong, I stand up straighter. I like that he's angry on my behalf. I like that he cares enough to be angry at all.

"Stupid fucker," Devon murmurs, pissed off. "You think he's at some bitch's place?"

"We don't have to call her unkind names," I say softly, sticking up for this hypothetical woman I created. "She doesn't owe me anything. If Josh cheated, he's the one in the wrong."

"Right," Mila agrees. "Plus, we don't know if she exists, or if Josh is guilty of cheating."

Devon and Axel exchange a look that confirms my hunch. As far as they're concerned, Josh is a cheater.

Axel sighs. "Where's St—"

Mila shakes her head, cutting him off. She wraps an arm around my waist and directs me to the kitchen island, where my full glass of water sits. "Don't you guys have a thing?" she asks, cryptically.

Axel frowns but Devon lifts his chin. Too deep into my feels to try to sort out their weird communication, I slide onto the barstool.

"Yep," Devon says, moving toward the door. "Keep your head up, Maisy."

I lift a hand in farewell.

Axel glances at me over his shoulder, his eyes burning, filled with so much anger, and regret, and a promise I don't know how to read. "I'll call you, Maisy."

I'm about to remind him he doesn't have my number, but the door closes and I lean back into the barstool, too tired to worry about semantics. What a day this has been. Right now, I don't feel strong or confident.

Brittle and weak, tired and hurting, are more accurate to describe the dull ache in my head and the heaviness tugging on my heart.

Mila sends a text before placing her phone facedown on the countertop. "You okay?"

My phone chirps and I close my eyes when I read the message.

Mom: How was your first day? I hope you made the right decision leaving the law firm, Maisy.

I snort and shrug. "Tomorrow will be better, right?"

Mila squeezes my hand. "Tomorrow will be so much better. I promise."

I give my best friend a smile and try to believe her.

————

AN HOUR PASSES. An hour where I speed track my way through the grieving process. I'm nearly reaching the acceptance stage when Mila's phone buzzes with a call. She takes it, turning away from the kitchen and entering the hallway near my bedroom.

Sighing, I slip off the barstool and wander into the living room. After swearing Josh out in anger, followed by a small slip into bargaining for his forgiveness, I spent the last ten minutes in a pity party of depression.

Please, someone, shake me out of this.

I stand at the edge of my living room and cross my arms over my chest.

The space appears larger now that it's bare. Furniture-less. Josh even swiped the rug. The lamp that once sat on a small table in my grandfather's study.

And, tears well in my eyes, my goldfish Lux.

"Who does that? Who steals a fucking goldfish?" I whirl

around, meeting Mila's surprised expression as she steps into the living room, her phone in her pocket.

"A dick," she answers.

"A jerk," I try for an insult.

"A pathetic excuse for a man."

"Right!" I punch the air but in the next moment, my tears spill over and I crumple to the floor because—I don't have a couch to crumple on!

My best friend sinks down next to me. "I'm sorry, Mais. I know Josh sucks and sure, he has a lazy streak that's miles, thousands of miles, long, but I never thought he'd steal your *furniture*."

"Or my goldfish," I sniffle.

"Or Lux," Mila agrees, looking around the empty space. "You know, it looks bigger."

"It does," I manage, a fresh wave of tears welling in my eyes.

"I like your dress," my friend says.

"That was the worst subject change I've ever heard. Ever hear of subtlety?"

She smirks. "Is it new?"

I laugh, running a hand over my face and shift closer to Mila. "I had a really bad day with really great moments."

Mila arches an eyebrow. "Does Axel Daire have anything to do with these great moments?"

I nod. "For appearing so rough and gruff, he really is a considerate man." I fill Mila in on the muffin debacle, followed by Axel's kindness, followed by my new dress and late breakfast.

"Wow," she says when I'm finished. "I didn't expect all that."

"Right? It was so nice, just for today, to feel like a man, who isn't my dad, really sees me." I pause, my eyelids growing heavy. My emotions have gone through the wringer today and I'm suddenly exhausted. Too drained to filter my thoughts. "I'm almost certain Josh was cheating on me," I voice the concern I know to be true in my heart. After months of his suspect behavior, followed by today, I'm sure my theory will be confirmed shortly. "And working for Tim...what a nightmare." I lean back, bracing my arms against the floor to support my weight. "But with Axel..."

"What?"

"It was nice, that's all. He was like a glimmer of hope on doomsday."

"I'm glad he was there for you today. You deserve to be with a good man, Maisy."

"A man like Axel?" I ask, half joking, half not.

Mila nods, her expression serious. "A man like Axel," she confirms my wish.

I yawn and Mila hugs me closer, tipping her head against mine. "You tired, Mais?"

"Exhausted."

"Why don't you get some sleep?"

"What time will the guys be back with dinner?" I ask. Or did they have to watch game tape or something? Devon and Axel took off right after Mila arrived and I didn't think to ask where they were going.

"Are you hungry?" Mila frowns.

"Not at all," I admit.

She squeezes my shoulder. "Go to sleep. I'll spend the night here and anything you need, just shout for me."

"Thanks," I agree so easily, I catch Mila off guard.

I hate asking for help, hate admitting defeat. But right now, my ego is bruised, my heart is wounded, and my soul—the very essence of my being—feels trampled on.

I know tomorrow will be better, brighter. Tomorrow, I'll

start my new job after manifesting from the top all over again.

But right now, I want cozy sweats and my pillow. I push off the floor and make my way toward my bedroom.

Mila has stayed at my house countless times. She'll make herself comfortable in the guest bedroom or, given the events of the day, crawl into bed beside me. I don't need to get her a pillow or remind her where the towels are.

The fact that she's barely a guest at all is comforting. Mila is my best friend and I feel better, stronger, with her spending the night. It's a relief to know I'm not alone. I slide out of the beautiful dress Axel bought me and place it carefully on a hanger.

Today sucked but there were moments...moments I need to hold on to and be grateful for.

I repeat this to myself, over and over, as I change into pajamas, brush my teeth, wash my face, and climb into bed. Staring at my crisp white ceiling, I force myself to recall all the blessings in my life until sleep claims me, tonight, the biggest blessing of all.

WHEN I WAKE in the morning, the air feels different. There's an energy, a newness that didn't exist when I cried myself to sleep the night before. From my bedroom, I hear the whirr of my coffee machine so Mila's already up. Stuffing my feet into slippers, I wade into the kitchen and stop short.

"What's this?" I gasp, my eyes widening as I take in my new living room.

My couch is back, along with the TV, Grandpa's lamp,

and—"Lux!" I exclaim, rushing to stare at my goldfish who couldn't care less about me.

Mila grins, passing me a coffee mug. "The guys tracked down Josh and reclaimed your stuff."

"Was he at Steve's?"

She nods, her eyes wide. "Josh hid from them in the bathroom."

I laugh with a deranged type of delight. "Coward."

"Totally!"

A new thought wriggles through my mind and I pause. "Was there another woman?"

Mila shakes her head, shrugging. "Not that I know of."

I narrow my gaze, but Mila's expression is just as uncertain as mine. She doesn't know.

I shake my head in disbelief. "I can't believe they did this for me. Wait, this is new." I point to an ivory pouf with big, black polka dots next to the couch. "And this!" I toe the rug with a very cool geometric pattern. "I didn't have a rug this big before."

Mila grins. "We thought we'd make a few improvements. Help make the space your own." *Now that Josh is gone.* She doesn't voice the words, but I hear them anyway.

I step into the living room, running my hand over the back of the couch, picking at the fringe of a new throw pillow. Laughter bubbles up from my throat. "I see you did some Feng Shui while you were at it."

"Lola even had Axel burn sage."

"What?" I shriek, spinning toward Mila.

She snorts. "I almost wish you were awake to hear how that play by play went down over speakerphone, but he really wanted to surprise you. We all did."

"I'm...surprised. And so damn thankful. Thank you. Thank all of y'all." I give Mila a big hug.

She pats my back. "It was mostly Axel."

"I can't believe it." I turn back toward the space, taking in my new living room. The small accents, the details, are all me and I devour them greedily, loving that this space finally feels like mine again after having Josh's boring ass occupy it for the better part of the last year.

"I can," Mila says quietly. "Axel's...protective of you."

"He's a good man," I say, giving a non-answer. Is he protective of me? Does Lola know about me because her friend, the server, filled her in? Or because there's something real to know?

Am I reading into things because yesterday was so awful and Axel comforted me? Did he do this because he feels sorry for me? Or because he cares more than he should?

And do I want him to? Can a man like Axel—successful, strong, larger than life—really look at me and see all the things most men, hell, even my own mother, overlook?

If he does, can I trust it enough to believe him?

FOUR
AXEL

"HEY, MAN." Devon drags a towel along the back of his neck and drops to the bench in the locker room.

We've just finished a morning skate, I've been awake since 3:30 AM, and I've slept like shit since Maisy Stratford re-entered my life as a single woman four days ago.

Has it really only been four days?

I squirt a stream of water into my mouth from my water bottle. "What's up?"

"Just wanted to say thanks. For helping out with Josh the other night. It was cool of you to go out of your way for Maisy like that and I appreciate it."

I narrow my eyes at my teammate. I know he's dating Maisy's best friend, Mila, and has developed his own friendship with Maisy. But it wasn't that long ago that I was having to help him pull his head out of his ass. He's not exactly Mr. Nice Guy who goes around helping women in need or looking out for anyone other than himself. And Mila.

And I guess, now Maisy.

"She really liked the new rug and stuff," Devon continues, missing my glare. "Mila says she hasn't had an easy year so..."

"So?" I flatten my expression.

Devon sighs and grips the back of his neck. "Just, don't lead her on, okay? It was cool of you—"

My hand clutches his practice jersey before he finishes that thought. "I don't need you to school me in how to treat women, hotshot." I call his bullshit out. "And certainly not women like Maisy."

Surprisingly, Hardt doesn't back down. Instead, he stands taller, his body locking down, his eyes narrowing. "What the fuck's that mean? Women like Maisy?"

"Good women," I growl. "Too fucking good." I give his jersey one final twist before I release him.

I lift an eyebrow, waiting for his reaction. No doubt, it will be a temper tantrum.

Instead, he laughs. He fucking cackles.

A few of the guys give us weird looks, but other than Barnes, who mutters some shit under his breath, the locker room clears out.

A month ago, if I pulled that shit with Devon, he would have decked me in the face. Now, he's staring at me like he knows a secret, something I don't, and he's fucking laughing.

I swear and stand, yanking open my locker door and pulling out a clean T-shirt.

"You like her," Devon states.

I turn to glare at him. "Of course, I like her. Who doesn't like Maisy?"

Devon shakes his head, rolling his lips together to conceal his laughter. "It's more than that. You *really* like her."

I swear again and sit back down.

Devon clasps my shoulder before thumping me once on the back. "I'm glad. She deserves to be with a decent man."

It's the nicest thing he's ever said to me but—"It's not like that. We're not together."

"Yet." Devon stands and rummages in his locker.

"Devon, her boyfriend broke up with her on Monday. I'm not looking to be a, a..." *Rebound.* I can't even say the word because of the sour taste it will leave in my mouth. Jesus, the thought is bad enough.

If Maisy Stratford, with her sweet smile and sparkling eyes, ever looked at me as a rebound, I couldn't stand it. She's the first woman who's inspired any reaction, any true feeling, in years and a dismissal by her would be more than rejection. It would *devastate* me.

"You're not her rebound," Devon clarifies. I wince at the word. "She and Josh have been over for a long time. This week just made it official." He turns and crosses his arms over his chest, his expression filled with disgust. "Did you see him with that girl?"

Anger burns through my veins at the memory. "He's such a sad suck," I spit out. When we caught up with Josh, he was crashing at the address Mila texted Devon. His friend Steve wasn't around, but his tongue was shoved so far down a random girl's throat, I'm surprised she didn't vomit in his mouth. My chest ached when I realized Maisy's hunch was correct. Josh is a cheater.

It was a nauseating display to witness, but it only got worse from there. "I thought he was going to piss himself," Devon recalls, smirking. "What a chump."

Upon seeing Devon and me, the little prick bolted from the room, barricading himself in Steve's bathroom and leaving his new plaything to stare up at us with wide eyes.

We're just here for some stuff, Devon told her pleasantly.

She shrugged, grabbed her purse, and took off. *Smart girl.*

Then, Devon and I had loaded up Maisy's belongings. I swore at Josh up and down when Devon got a text from Mila about the fucking goldfish, and we left.

Josh never came out of the bathroom. I'm not sure if his cowardice eased some of my anger or escalated it. On one hand, I'm certain Maisy will never take him back. On the other, he got off too damn easy.

"How's she doing?" I ask, pulling off my jersey.

Devon shrugs. "She's okay. I think the new job and having a routine have helped. Mila spent the night at Maisy's last night. Their friendship is rock solid. I wish I had someone I could count on like that. Besides Mila."

"Hm," I grunt, knowing exactly what he means. Sure, I have my brother, Asher. But he's usually spearfishing or skydiving, too busy chasing a thrill, to deal with my mundane bullshit. However, if I really need him, he'll drop everything to show up for Lola and me.

I've been on a few hockey teams during my long career, but I've never had that connection. A person I can regularly count on for the day-to-day shit.

Well, that's not entirely true. I have Lola. But she's my kid and as close as we are, there are obviously things I can't rely on her for.

Damn. Maybe Lola and Asher are right. I have been on my own too long. I do need to try harder to make *friends*. To seek fucking happiness.

"Just, keep an eye on her." I stand and close my locker door.

Devon snorts. "Yeah. You too." He gives me a pointed look that I ignore.

Making my way out of the locker room, I nearly collide

with one of the wingers, River Patton. The guy who can't check his damn anger and nearly knocked Maisy over her first day of work.

"You." I point at him.

He scowls but stops and looks at me.

"Apologize to Maisy Stratford. Show her, and every woman, and man," I tack on for good measure, "working for this team some goddamn respect. You hear me?"

River's face is stone, his eyes flat. He rolls his lips together and I wait for him to unleash some of his pent-up anger my way. I've witnessed a handful of his meltdowns over the summer, and they increased my dislike of the kid. River surprises me though; he nods.

"Good." I walk away. I thought putting the kid in his place would feel better than it does. I'm still annoyed. Keyed up.

When I pass by the front office, I pause, glancing through the large windows.

Maisy's sitting at a desk inside, casually chatting with Betty. Her hair is pulled back into a low bun at the nape of her neck, a few strands escaping and framing her face. Her lips are painted a sweet pink. She's wearing another sundress, this one green with ruffles at the sleeves.

She's beautiful. Stunning. Smart and sophisticated.

Maisy isn't a woman I can try casual with. She deserves the best, my best. But casual is all I know how to do. How pathetic is that? At thirty-six-years old, I don't know the first thing about dating. I don't know the first thing about being in a committed, romantic relationship.

As if she feels me staring, she turns. Our eyes meet and I note the surprise in her gaze. She pats at her hair nervously, her tongue swiping a path over her lower lip.

The visual, as simple and innocent as it is, affects me. I practically press my nose against the damn glass.

But I can't look away. I don't want to.

I want to give Maisy my best, all of me. Even the parts I forgot exist.

But can I risk it? Can I open myself up to a woman whose entire life is in upheaval?

She jumps, startled, as someone calls her name.

As she turns in the direction of the door, my eyes follow.

Fucking River Patton. He either just cock blocked me or saved me and both options annoy me.

I back away from the window as River talks to Maisy.

I need to get a grip. I need to check my desire for this woman and approach her, this, the right way. Slowly, thoughtfully, carefully.

Maisy's been hurt too much in the past for me to blaze into her life when it's already been flipped upside down.

And I don't know how to navigate all the feelings she inspires inside me.

With her, I need to take my time. I need to think things through. It has to be careful and measured.

Basically, I need to proceed with caution. For both of us.

FIVE
MAISY

MY LIFE SETTLES into a new norm. After the initial shock of Josh's deceit, along with the gushy photos he posted of himself on Instagram, pictured with different women, half drunk with glazed eyes, sliding off a barstool at Corks, I realize how much better off I am.

Why did I stay in a one-sided relationship for as long as I did? Why did I allow myself to internalize Josh's barbed words and backhanded compliments for as long as I have?

I'm strong and confident. I've worked hard, with the help of Dad, Missy, and Mila, to find self-worth in the wake of my mom's barbed words, Tim Clancy's hurtful remarks, and a string of unfulfilling relationships. I deserve more, at least what I invest, and Josh never gave me half of that.

As the weeks roll into each other and I find my footing with the Tennessee Thunderbolts, everything improves. It's easier to wake up in the mornings and take a brisk walk, clearing my mind and mentally organizing my day. I enjoy my morning coffee, sitting in my beautiful living room with pops of bright color, reading the news on my phone.

I buy Lux some new rocks for her fish tank and spruce

up the succulents on the windowsill in my kitchen. I join my sister for more happy hours and head over to my parents' house for Sunday dinners or a weekend coffee.

Slowly, I take back pieces of myself that I lost. Parts of my personality I loved before Josh drove them into the ground. Before Tim belittled my intelligence and swiped at my confidence. Before they both amplified the insecurities my mother saddled me with during my teenage years, when she constantly, maybe unknowingly, compared my figure, my grades, *me*, to Missy.

I realize that the way I was living wasn't living at all. I was existing, getting through one day just to make it through another. My hours were stuffed with never-ending tasks that resulted in hurtful comments and disappointment.

Now, I'm digging myself out of that gloomy place. I'm realizing how great it can be. Living. Having the freedom to order out on a Monday night just because I'm craving fish tacos or watch whatever I want on Netflix without consulting someone else. I can invite my sister to sleep over and stay up late, drinking wine and watching old movies. I love the peace of mind, the clarity, I possess when I used to be filled with self-doubt and anxiety. Overanalyze much? I did.

And now, I don't have to, and it feels so good. Liberating. Finally, I see what Dad's been trying to show me for years; I understand the motivation behind Mila's pep talks. I value the gift of manifestation my college professor introduced me to. For once, I'm living the life they constantly reminded me I was capable of choosing.

I'm walking into The Honeycomb on a Monday, a hot coffee in hand, a whistle on my lips, when I nearly run into River Patton.

"Morning, River," I say, smiling at him. He's young,

gruff, and has the biggest chip on his shoulder I've ever encountered. But when he came to apologize to me my first week with the Bolts, he was sincere. For that alone, I cut him some slack and over the past few weeks, we've become acquaintances.

"Hey, Mais," he greets me. "Why the hell you whistling?"

"Because it's Monday."

"Exactly," he mutters sarcastically.

"We've got the whole week ahead of us. It's like starting with a clean slate."

River shoots me a bewildered look. I smile at him and after a moment, he shakes his head and groans out, "You're too damn sunny, Maisy."

"You're welcome," I toss back, walking into the office.

When I enter, with River on my heels, I pull up short when I spot Axel waiting at my desk. In fact, he's seated right in front of it, looking at his phone.

"Hey!" I say.

He looks up, his expression clearing for a beat when he notices me, and then darkening again when he sees River. Uh-oh, I'll have to tell Axel that River apologized and we're good.

"See you later, Mais." River smartly removes himself from the situation.

I round my desk, drop my purse in the corner, and sit down.

"How are you?" I ask Axel.

"Good," he says gruffly. "You?"

"Much better. Thank you, Axel, for...everything. I meant to call you, but I don't have your number and haven't seen you around." I inch closer and drop my tone. "I've never had anyone stand up for me the way you and Devon did. It meant a lot."

Axel clears his throat, looking around the space uncomfortably. Right now, we're the only two people in the office since Betty is most likely preparing her coffee in the kitchen. Of course, I've seen him since my first week of work but never alone, never where I could thank him for all he did for me.

"It was nothing."

"It was something," I counter, wanting him to know how touched I was by his actions. The past few weeks have been a whirlwind and I've tried to seek Axel out a few times but have never managed to come face to face with him, just the two of us. Until now.

"You're welcome," he says finally, tugging on the back of his neck. "I'm, uh, hoping you can help me with something." He pulls out his wallet and drops his license and insurance cards on the desk.

"Sure," I say, switching back into work mode. I fire up my computer and log in, picking up Axel's cards. I grin. "Your middle name is Raphael?"

"After the painter," he says glumly.

"Seriously?"

"My mom was an artist."

"Oh my God, that's so cool!" I wait for more details and receive none. "Please, tell me more..."

He does that thing where he looks like he's going to smile, but his lip falls at the last second. "There's not much to tell. Mom studied art history before giving painting a go. She lived in this little studio in the Village in New York for most of the sixties." He snorts. "The stories she used to tell... She would have loved you."

His use of the past tense slams into me. "She passed?"

He nods, a streak of anguish blazing across his face. "Both of my parents, a few years back."

"I'm sorry."

"Me too." He clears his throat.

Sensing he doesn't want to talk about it, I stack his cards and tap them against the desk. "What are these for?"

"Oh, right." He shakes his head, as if clearing it. "I need to add Lola to my health insurance. She was under her mom's plan when she started at UT because she had better coverage here than my plan offered. But now that I'm a resident of Tennessee, my coverage is more comprehensive."

"Sure," I say easily, reaching into my drawer to pull out a paper. "Can you fill out this form? And then, just send me a copy of her ID when you have a chance."

He takes the slip of paper and I pass him a pen. Head bent, Axel fills out the information. I study him. The fullness of his eyebrows, the thickness of his hair. Everything is...rich. A chocolate, espresso color that contains a fullness that is so manly, my body tightens from his proximity.

His handwriting is slightly slanted but bold, just like him. He writes in all caps and it makes me smile because he's the opposite of shouty. He's quiet and perceptive, often unnerving.

"Do I have something in my hair?" he asks quietly.

"What?"

He looks up, his eyes amused. "You're staring."

"Oh." I sit up straight, feeling my cheeks burn for being obvious. For being called out.

Axel's expression softens. "Are you coming out for the Rookie's birthday?"

"Cole Philips?"

Axel looks like he's trying not to laugh. I'm not much of

a hockey girl and I only know Cole's the rookie because the whole team calls him Rookie. "That's the one."

I grin cheekily. "Har har. But no, I'm not going. I don't really know him and—"

"You should come."

I wrinkle my nose. Axel stares back.

"Won't that be strange? I mean, we've met a few times but we're not friends and—"

"You're part of the Bolts, Maisy. He'd be happy to have you," Axel responds decisively.

"You think so?"

At my wariness, Axel's expression softens, tenderness sweeping his gaze. "I know so. Come. We're just doing dinner and getting drinks at Corks."

"I can't make dinner. I have a late meeting with Betty, but drinks sound good."

"Want a ride? I can pick you up?"

At his offer, a shiver rolls down my spine. Is he offering to be nice, because my house is on the way to Corks? Or because he *wants* to pick me up? There's a difference and I desperately want his reason to be the second scenario.

"Okay," I agree.

Axel smiles. He actually smiles with both sides of his mouth, and it renders me speechless. His teeth are a pearly white, a sharp contrast against the dark brown of his beard. And oh my, he is gorgeous. Not just hot or gruff or burly. When Axel smiles, he exudes all the warmth he keeps under wraps and it's sexy. "Okay. I'll swing by around 8:30. Here, give me your number. If I'm running late, I'll message."

I smile back, knowing what he's doing. He's *flirting* with me. He *wants* to pick me up; he *wants* my number.

I rattle it off and try not to squee when my phone chirps

with a text from him, sharing his number.

Instead, I busy myself with scanning his cards and paperwork. I pass him the cards. "Once you send me Lola's ID, I'll get her added to your insurance."

"Great. Thanks, Maisy. I'll see you tonight."

"See you," I say, watching him leave the office.

"Whew! That was some smolder," Betty announces.

My head whips in her direction and I burst out laughing when I notice her sitting at her desk, fanning herself with a paper plate.

"Betty! I didn't hear you come in."

"How could you with all that man muscle looking at you like a snack?" she responds reasonably.

"Oh God!" My palms slap over my bright red cheeks.

Betty laughs and shakes her head. "He's a good one, doll. Too serious, but as good-hearted as they come."

I nod, knowing exactly what she means.

Axel isn't showy like Devon. He's not a goofball like Damien Barnes or sullen and moody like River. He's just quiet, perceptive, and *real*.

But he's got a big heart and big hands and right now, I want them both.

Betty reaches over and passes me a plate. I join her, fanning myself, as the color in my cheeks recedes and my blood pressure normalizes.

But my heart skips another beat, and my thoughts stay tangled up on Axel, and tonight, for the rest of the day.

———

IF THERE EVER WAS A BIRTHDAY TO crash, it would be the Rookie's. Cole Philips is one of the nicest, most down to earth, innocent guys on the team. He's thoughtful, kind, and considerate. In many ways, he reminds me of a younger Axel but, surprisingly, the guy on the team who has taken Cole under his wing is Devon.

As such, Mila is attending Cole's birthday dinner and drinks and knowing that my best friend will be nearby eases some of the nerves in my stomach as 8:30 PM ticks nearer.

Hanging with the Bolts is good for me. For sure, it's an ego boost, to be surrounded by so many wildly attractive and larger than life athletes who could pummel Josh with their pinkie fingers. But it's more than that. When I'm with them, I feel protected. There's a sense of security that's been present from the beginning, right when Mila met Devon, that all the guys extended to both of us. At first, I thought their kindness and concern toward me was because I'm Mila's friend. That may be part of it, but it's not all of it. Because the inclusivity I've felt from the Bolts is more than what I experienced from the Knoxville Coyotes.

When Mila dated star quarterback Avery Callaway, the other players were nice. They tolerated my presence and, except for Cohen who became a sincere and close friend, only made small talk on occasion. But I wasn't one of them, never truly in the fold. They didn't invite me to birthday dinners or seek me out to say hello at team events I attended.

With the Bolts, it already feels different. I belong in a way I never did with the Coyotes. Maybe it's because I now work in HR, but I felt the connection before starting my new job. The realization of both eases and heightens my nerves about tonight.

I want Axel to like me because of how much I admire him. But I also want Axel to like me because I want a chance of belonging to the Thunderbolts the way Mila does. Fully.

SIX

AXEL

"SO, IT'S A DATE." Lola bounces on the edge of my bed, staring at me.

I meet her eyes in the reflection of the mirror. "It's not a date."

She rolls her eyes. "What would you call taking out a woman—the same woman you took for breakfast a few weeks ago—for drinks?"

"Attending a friend's birthday party," I clarify, my voice gruff.

Lola snorts, wrinkling her adorable nose she inherited from my mother. "Dad, I need details. All Jas told me—"

"Jas exaggerates." I run my fingers through my hair, wondering if I need a trim. I turn a little, gauging the length before pulling it back into a bun.

"You need a trim," Lola informs me. "And true, she does. But I don't think she is about this."

I sigh, turning to face my daughter. Sometimes, I look at her and she's still a four-year-old kid. She's got a big gap from missing three of her four front teeth and is wearing multicolored butterfly clips in her hair.

Now, she's beautiful. Smart, motivated, talented. She cares more about school than I ever did and the fact that she's one of only seven women in her coding cohort fills me with more emotions than I can process.

When the hell did that happen? When did Lola grow up?

"Dad."

I shake my head, blinking away the mist that clouds my eyes. "Huh?"

"Jas isn't wrong about this."

I sigh, moving to my closet to pick out a shirt. I never put this much thought into my appearance—I'm *not* Devon Hardt—but tonight, I want to look nice. Put together.

"What's Maisy's last name?" Lola follows me.

"Stratford. Maisy Stratford."

"Cute!"

I side-eye my kid and she grins.

"And you asked her out?"

"I offered to give her a ride to Cole's birthday drinks."

Lola's gaze narrows. "But not dinner."

"She was busy."

"With what?" Lola crosses her arms over her chest. Ah, so protective, my girl. She gets it from me.

"She just started a new job—"

"With the Bolts."

"Yes. And she had a late meeting."

Lola nods slowly, digesting this information. "Is she a drinker?"

"What?" I glare.

"Is that why you offered to DD?"

"Don't you have homework?"

My daughter laughs. "You just want to drive her home."

I pull gray and blue shirts off the hangers, but Lola takes

the gray one from my hand and re-hangs it. "Wear the navy. Sometimes you look washed out in pewter gray."

"Huh?"

"Did you tell Uncle Asher about her?"

"There's nothing to tell."

She smacks me in the stomach and moves back to my bed. "Sooo, do I need to give you the talk?"

"Lola," I growl.

She cracks up. "All right, all right." She stands from the bed. "I gotta get going anyway. Have fun tonight, Daddy. I mean it." She pauses until I look up and catch her gaze. "You deserve to be happy, big guy. And I haven't seen you like this"—she gestures toward me fretting over freaking navy or pewter—"in a long time. It's a good look. Uncle Asher will be happy for you too."

I soften immediately. It means more than I can express that Lola would be okay with me dating, or not dating but being open to the idea of dating. If she has any reservations, I'd shut it down immediately.

The fact that she's excited for me, makes me excited about tonight. So much so, that I hope dinner flies by so I can scoop up Maisy and head to Corks.

"Where are you doing dinner?" Lola asks as she shoulders her computer bag.

"Clint's," I say, naming an upscale sports bar.

She clucks her tongue. "Fancy. And Corks for drinks?"

I nod, buttoning up my shirt over my white undershirt Lola gives me shit for wearing. She says they're old-fashioned.

At her silence, I look up again, my stomach dropping when I note the glimmer in her eyes.

"No," I shut it down.

She snorts. "I'm twenty-one now, big guy."

"Lorisse Marie—"

"You're full-naming me?"

"Do not show up at Corks tonight."

She laughs. Evilly. She gets that from me too. Me and Asher.

"I'm serious." I point at her, trying to look stern.

She rolls her eyes. "See you later, big guy."

Lola leaves my room and a moment later, I hear the front door close.

As much as I pretend she breaks my balls, I love Lola more than life. Would she and Maisy hit it off? Would they bond and have some type of friendship between them?

It's way too early for Maisy to meet her. Logically, I know that. Nah, Lola won't swing by the bar. She's just breaking my balls. I'm sure she already has plans with Jasmine. I blow out a breath, relieved Lola is just giving me grief.

I stare at my reflection in the mirror. My beard is neatly trimmed. My brown eyes are so dark, they look black. Just like my kid's. And dammit, she was right. I do look better in navy.

I hope Maisy thinks so too.

———

DINNER AT CLINT'S is easygoing and chill. Cole's genuinely touched that the team wanted to get together and take him out for his birthday and it shows. He's an endearing kid and I'm far enough removed from my early days of playing to note that his approach—sincere and solid —will assist him in his career more than the hot-headed approach I've seen too many rookies exhibit over the years.

Nah, Cole's a good kid and raising a glass in honor of his

twenty-fourth birthday feels right. Most of the team assembled, with Devon and Mila looking like a power couple, and Beau Turner showing up with his Gran. Unfortunately, she forgot to turn off the stove and nearly burned down the house last week. Now, he's too nervous to leave her on her own and is counting down the weeks for his little sister to move back home and share some of the caretaking responsibilities with him. Damien strolls in late, turning the head of nearly every woman in the place. And River, well, he sulks like usual.

All in all, it's a great dinner but when the bill is settled and the team splits up into different rides to head to Corks, I'm relieved. I can't wait to see Maisy, and the low-key atmosphere of Corks, coupled with Cole's birthday, takes a lot of pressure off.

When I slide behind the wheel of my ride, I send her a message.

Me: Be there in ten.

Maisy: Okay. See you soon.

I grin that she spelled out "okay." Used to Lola's abbreviations, sometimes she doesn't even use words, just emojis, the direct text is appreciated. Who the hell knows what a skull followed by a man running is supposed to mean anyway?

I pull away from Clint's and head toward Maisy's place. The closer I get, the more excited I feel. Anticipation snakes its way through my limbs, my stomach knots and loops. I haven't felt this way in a long time. Years. Fuck, decades.

With Maisy, I can envision more. Some kind of future. Being Lola's dad has been the driving force of every decision I've made for the last two decades. For the first time in my adulthood, I'm at a place where I can date for me.

Where I can find happiness for myself and, for the most part, put my own needs and wants first.

It's an unsettling thought but it also opens a door of possibilities I haven't considered. Can I have a real relationship with Maisy Stratford? Can we build something real? Something like my parents had? Or Anna and Ben have now?

I tap my palm against the steering wheel, my mind racing. Does she think tonight is a date? Will she expect me to kiss her when I drop her off? Does she want me to kiss her or is that too forward? Presumptuous?

Shit. I should have asked Lola, or Jas, what the damn rules are now.

No, I can't ask them. I should ask Asher.

Lola was right; I need to tell my brother. He'll be excited for this new development in my life and offer more advice and tips than necessary. Damn, I wish I already reached out to him.

I don't know what I'm doing. Dating is so far out of my wheelhouse, I start to panic. What I thought was low-key birthday drinks for Cole, could also be construed as a cop-out, right?

Why didn't I just pick up the phone and ask her out? Like a man?

By the time I pull in front of Maisy's house, the back of my neck tingles and the knots in my stomach feel unbearable.

I park the car and step out, taking a few deep breaths as I walk toward her front door.

Before I step onto the porch, the yellow door swings open and Maisy steps outside.

I gulp, my throat drying. Every thought I had a moment ago fades away. My nerves dissipate and I stop, standing still to gaze at the most breathtakingly beautiful woman I've ever laid eyes on.

Her blonde hair is pulled back in a low bun, with a few curls escaping to frame her face. Her makeup is subtle, but her eyes look bigger, popping bright blue. She's wearing a flirty summer dress that ruffles above her knees and trails longer in the back. But it's her smile that's the knockout.

Because she's looking at me—*smiling* at me—like I'm the man she's been waiting on. Not just for tonight. But for years.

The same way I've been waiting on her.

I clear my throat. "You look beautiful."

At the rawness of my tone, her expression softens.

"You clean up nice too, Axe," she says, tipping her head to the side.

I clear my throat again, give half a chuckle. "Yeah, thanks," I manage.

Maisy's smile grows. "Thanks for picking me up. You didn't have to go out of your way."

"It's no trouble. You're on the way." I tip my head to the car. "You ready?"

She stares at me for a long moment, as if making up her mind about something. Then, she takes a deep inhale and slowly releases it. "Yes, I'm ready."

We turn toward my truck together. By the time she's strapped in and I'm driving to Corks, the door of possibilities has widened. Suddenly, everything seems within reach.

I look over at Maisy and smile.

Absolutely everything.

SEVEN

MAISY

I'VE SPENT a lot of time at Corks. First, as a UT student, when Corks still had $0.25 shots on Tuesday nights, although no one ever confirmed what was in them. Then, when the Coyotes took over the bar in my early twenties, I hung here with Mila on weekends.

But when I enter now, on the arm of Axel Daire, the atmosphere is different. I'm not just in a college bar or killing time with my bestie and her boyfriend. Instead, I'm here because there's nowhere else I'd rather be. There's no other guy I'd rather spend time getting to know.

"You made it!" Mila calls when Axel and I reach the bar.

I give a little wave before she wraps me in a hug. "You look hot," she whispers in my ear.

My smile widens. I've played it safe—cardigans and taupe eye shadow—for too long. Ever since I made my peace with Josh, I've been embracing change more. And tonight, a swipe of pink lipstick and a summer dress makes me feel like myself. A more enhanced, happier version than I've been the past few years.

"Hey, Mais! I got your drink." Damien grins, gesturing at the bartender.

I open my mouth to tell him I'll take a margarita when I hear him call out. "A margarita, salt on the rim." He orders a local beer for Axel, and it hits me how much these guys, this team, have welcomed me into their circle.

"Maisy!" The birthday boy smiles when he sees me. It's big and genuine and crushes my lingering doubt about crashing his party. Cole slugs an arm around my shoulders. "Thanks for coming."

I reach up on my tippytoes to hug him back. "Happy birthday, Cole."

River slips off a barstool and tips his head for me to take it. I give him a grateful smile and slide onto the seat, feeling Mila's and Axel's and a lot of eyes on me.

"What?" I ask Mila.

She shakes her head, biting her lip as she studies me. "You're the team's sweetheart."

I laugh.

She grins. "You seem different."

I lift an eyebrow. "You want to psychoanalyze now?" My eyes sweep the crowded bar.

"No," Mila laughs. "I just mean, I'm happy you came out, Mais. You look *happy*."

I glance around at the guys, drink in the laughter and jokes. I take in the bar, bustling and noisy. When I look at Axel, I nearly drown in the heat flaring in his eyes. And I love that it's offset by a flicker of protectiveness. *For me.*

Tonight, I don't feel like an outsider in a group of friends. I don't feel like the outcast, hanging on the periphery. Or the shorter, rounder Stratford sister. I'm here, people are happy to see me, and it's an *acceptance* I haven't known before.

"I am," I say quietly.

Mila nods, understanding lining her face. "Good."

"Here you go." Damien passes me a margarita.

"Thanks, Damien." I lift it in his direction before clinking it against Mila's and taking a sip.

Mila and I make small talk as I watch Axel interact with his teammates. He doesn't have the easygoing affability of Damien. He's not sour and surly like River. He's doesn't exude edgy hotheadedness like Devon.

Axel's the mature man on the team. He looks every bit the Brawler he's known to be, but his demeanor speaks to a wisdom, an edge, that the other men don't possess. He'll rumble if need be, but he'd rather not if a few words will suffice. He'll step up if he has to, but don't waste his time. He knows who he is, what he wants, and is willing to do what it takes to ensure success—but never at the expense of someone else.

The fact that he's giving me attention, a woman trying to find her footing after swimming in a pool of self-doubt and insecurity for too long, is exhilarating. It fills me with a confidence that my other encounters with men always lacked.

When Axel looks around for me, he doesn't do it to make sure I'm keeping tabs on him, the way Josh did. Instead, Axel looks around for me because he's looking for me. And when his eyes catch mine, he excuses himself from the conversation with Devon and steps to the barstool I'm perched on.

"Are you happy you came?" he asks, his eyebrows pulling together.

The smile I give him must exude reassurance because the line between his brows disappears and he gives me a lazy, half-smirk.

"I really am," I confirm.

"Good." He plants one huge hand on my knee. "I am too." He watches me for a beat before adding, "I've never done this before."

I wait for him to continue, but when he says nothing I prod, "Done what?"

He clears his throat, ducking his head as if embarrassed. "Brought a woman to a team thing."

"Oh." I tilt my head, wondering if he means this summer with the Bolts, or before when he played for the Seattle Rams.

"Ever." His voice is thick, as if he's admitting something he'd rather not. As if he can hear the question I didn't voice.

"Huh?" I blurt out, wincing at how incredulous I sound. But...what? He's never brought a woman to a team thing in his fifteen-year career?

I didn't think it was possible for a man like Axel, with his size and bulk and general toughness, to become easily flustered. I was wrong. Axel's cheeks heat and his eyes dart around the bar, clearly out of his comfort zone. It's adorable and endearing more than anything else.

To ease his mind, I place my hand on top of his, pressing the warmth of his palm into my knee.

I wait patiently, my eyes glued to his face, until he meets my gaze and works a swallow.

"I mean, a few times, from when I was in a relationship. But that was over a decade ago. Before Seattle. I don't...do this." He looks away again. "Shit."

I frown, trying to follow his line of thought. Does he regret bringing me? Is it too much, too soon?

"Lola's here." He snorts, shaking his head. "She's trying to be a little sneak." He heaves out a sigh, looking half frustrated, half amused. "You up for meeting my kid?"

My eyes widen as I try to keep up with the shifting conversation. Gone are my thoughts of too much, too soon. Because he's asking me if I want to meet his daughter?

Granted, she's a fully-grown adult and—

"Lola!" He waves a hand in the air, his voice booming.

I turn to see a beautiful woman blush a bright shade of red and try to duck behind a pinball machine.

Next to me, Mila cracks up. By now, Devon is standing in our circle along with Damien and Cole.

"Don't call her out, man," Damien advises.

"She's embarrassed," Cole confirms.

"I would be too if my grandpa was flagging me down like this," River cuts in.

Axel gives him a dirty look and waves his hand again, more obvious this time. "Lorisse Daire, I see you!"

Mila groans and I sink down a bit on the barstool. Poor girl is really getting called out now, with other patrons glancing in her direction.

I recognize the server from the cafe, Jasmine, and grin. Jasmine pulls a bright-faced and obviously mortified Lola from behind the pinball machine and toward our waiting huddle.

"You are so fucking embarrassing," River mutters.

"I never thought I'd agree with Patton, but he's right," Devon adds.

"Hey, D!" Jasmine calls out, punching Axel in the arm.

Axel gives her a look but doesn't comment. His words are for Lola. "What the hell are you doing hiding being a pinball machine? Stop being a weirdo and come say hello to your father like the respectable woman I raised you to be."

"Damn," Jas whispers. "It's like that, Lol."

Now that Lola is standing before us, with nowhere to hide and nowhere to go, her demeanor shifts. I see the exact moment she decides to own this introduction because the color fades from her cheeks and she straightens her spine. After drawing in a deep inhale, she sticks her hand in my direction and announces, "I'm Lola Daire."

"Maisy Stratford," I say, shaking her hand. "It's a pleasure to meet you, Lola."

"I feel like this is a big moment," Damien murmurs.

"Totally," Mila agrees, slurping her margarita like she's tuning into an episode of *The Kardashians*. She shakes her empty glass at Devon, the ice rattling, and he sighs, shifting over to the bar to order her a refill. "Keep going."

Lola grins. "I was jealous my best friend met you before I did."

Axel guffaws and Jasmine rolls her eyes.

But I like that Lola is being upfront and honest. After years of never quite belonging, I appreciate her direct approach.

"Well, I'm glad you came to meet me for yourself," I admit. "I didn't really have time to overthink how this could go," I add, gesturing between us, "and now I'm glad because the moment is here, we're doing it, and you should pull up a barstool and have a drink."

I glance at Axel, wondering if it'd be weird for Lola to have a drink with us, with the Bolts, but she's in Corks so...

"I'll take a margarita." She slips onto the stool beside mine.

"Make it two." Jasmine grins.

River smirks. "I like these girls."

Axel gives him a look that's a clear warning and gestures to the bartender. Once the girls have fresh margaritas in front of them, I lift my glass and clink it against Lola's.

"Tell me about yourself, Lola Daire."

She gives the same half-smile as her dad, not giving an inch. "You first, Maisy Stratford."

"Damn," Jasmine mutters.

River rubs his hands together, his elbows dropping to the bar on the other side of Mila. He leans forward to watch my exchange with Lola. Behind me, I feel Axel's presence, unsure how close to get, when to intervene, or if he should just let this moment play out.

But I'm enjoying it. I like Lola's spunk. I wish I had more of it.

"I just got out of a shitty relationship," I admit, surprising the whole bar. "He was cheating."

"What a dick," Lola sputters, disgust heavy in her tone.

"You knew he was cheating?" Devon asks.

Mila and I both whip our heads toward him. When he shoots Axel a helpless look, Mila, Lola, Jasmine, and my eyes follow.

"Shit." River shakes his head, trying to disguise his laughter by coughing.

Axel holds up two hands and shuffles back two steps. "We thought you knew. I mean, when we went to get your furniture, he was with that girl but—"

"Axel, check out this game," Cole interrupts, pointing to one of the televisions over the bar, and saving his teammate. Even on his birthday, Cole Philips is a stand-up guy.

Whatever.

The girls and I turn back to each other.

"I'm in the coding program, studying computer science," Lola admits, taking a long pull of her drink. She shoots her dad a look but given how far away he now is, she feels it's safe to continue. "So, no one wants to date me." She wrinkles her nose. "Too nerdy."

Jasmine nods in confirmation.

"They'll outgrow that when you can hack into their social media accounts," I offer.

"True. Story." Jasmine's eyes widen as she looks at me again.

Lola rolls her lips together, waiting for me to give another detail about myself.

"I just started a new job with the Thunderbolts. Human Resources. I like to craft, cross-stitch, paint, make pottery—anything to keep my hands busy. It helps me think. I take walks in the morning. Drink way too much coffee. Oh, and I'm trying to add more color into my wardrobe."

Lola nods, her eyes holding mine. "Do you like *Grey's Anatomy*?"

"Um, yeah." I give her a look, surprised by the throwback. Is that what college kids are watching these days? "Meredith Grey is my spirit sister."

Slowly, a smile works across Lola's face. She picks up her margarita and clinks it against mine, taking another long sip, until she nearly drains it. "I'm glad you're dating my dad." She slips off her barstool.

"Well, I'm not sure if we're da—"

"He could use more color in his wardrobe too. Be good to him," she cuts me off before I can backpedal. Then, she's ducking back into the crowd, disappearing from view with Jasmine trailing behind her.

I turn toward Mila. "What just happened?"

"I think you just got her seal of approval," my best friend says, her own approval evident in her tone.

"You did," River agrees, finishing his beer. "It was pretty fucking cool."

"It was, wasn't it?" I ask, impressed with my own ability to pull that off.

I spin on my barstool and search for Axel. When I find

him, he gives me the biggest smile I've ever seen him sport and my heart skips a beat.

Maybe we are dating. Maybe this is the sign from the universe I've been waiting on.

And River was right; it was pretty fucking cool. I started tonight wondering if Axel and I were going on a date and now...I'm wondering if we have a shot at a future.

EIGHT
AXEL

"I DIDN'T KNOW Lola was going to show up," I tell Maisy, worried Lola came on too strong. My daughter is intelligent, witty, and the most important woman in my life. As much as she says she wants me to date, saying something and experiencing it are two vastly different concepts. "I mean, she hinted at it, but I thought she was joking. If I thought she was going to show, I would have given you a heads-up."

"It definitely broke the ice," Maisy laughs, looking more relaxed than worried. She shrugs. "She's just looking out for you."

I tip my head in concession of her point. "It's only been me and Lola for a long time."

Maisy nods, understanding lightening her eyes. "I'm glad we met. She's awesome."

I smile at the sincerity underlining her words. "Yeah, she's awesome. Also, drives me nuts. She hasn't caught on that I don't need looking after."

Maisy bites her bottom lip. "Don't you?"

A rumble of laughter moves through my chest,

surprising me since I don't laugh often. At least not with women other than Lola and Jas. I glance down at my dark jeans and plain blue shirt. My dark hair is pulled back, a messy knot at the back of my head. I shrug.

Maisy laughs, reaching for my forearm playfully. But she hangs on once she catches it, her fingernails grazing my skin. "I didn't mean your appearance, Axel. You've got this sexy, understated, Jason Momoa look going on."

My eyebrows nearly disappear into my hairline. Jason Momoa? "Aquaman?"

Maisy giggles. God, she's adorable. And sweet. And too fucking nice to compare me to a DC Comics character. "I bet Lola would agree."

"Jas, maybe," I concede. "Lol would cringe."

Maisy dips her head. I'm not sure if it's in agreement or embarrassment, but her cheeks are flushed, her eyes bright, and she blossoms before me. The energy between us shifts. More flirtation, less uncertainty. More possibility, less questioning.

The graze of her fingernails stops, holding still but with more of a grip. I shift closer and she crosses her legs, until her hip is nearly pressing into my side. I hang onto the bar, and she slides her hand farther up my arm. Her palm is smooth and the sensation of her skin against mine causes a thrill to shoot through me.

I haven't been a saint. I've slept with women over the past decade. But rarely the same woman. And never more than two or three times.

With Maisy, it's different. I'd want more than a handful of nights. I'd want...more with her. It should scare me but I'm too old to not know my own mind. As much as Lola's presence annoyed me at first, now, it's a blessing. Because Lola's approval of Maisy gives me the nudge I need to make a move. God, I want to kiss her. To show her how I feel, even if I can't say it.

I'm peering down at her, our eyes locked, silently feeling each other out. I note the same desire coursing through my veins, rippling over her expression. I see the questions burning behind her irises. She wants reassurances.

For the first time in years, I want to give them to her. I lower my face to her ear. "Yes, Maisy."

"What?" she gasps, half a question, half a wish.

I smile and the curve of my lip runs along the shell of her ear. "I want to kiss you."

She stills but her chest rises and falls faster. I turn my head, my mouth nearly running along her jaw. A moment of hesitation sparks in my mind and I pause.

I can't kiss Maisy here. In front of all these people. The Bolts, the Coyotes, the patrons of Corks.

My molars grind together. But God, do I want to. I want to lay her out on the damn bar and kiss her fiercely, possessively, enough to show everyone in here that I more than like her. Already, I care about her.

She lifts her face, her eyes wide, curious, hopeful.

"Maisy—" I whisper.

"Shots!" A voice rings out behind me.

Cole Philips knocks into us from the side and my arm darts out to keep Maisy upright on the barstool as I'm shoved into her.

I shake Philips off, about to cuss him out for being so damn careless. But the second I turn, I realize how drunk he is. It's his birthday and he's the damn rookie, green and eager and too damn nice.

"I'm sorry, Brawler," he slurs, his eyes glazed as they land on the empty glass in his hand. "I never drink this much. Ever." He looks back up at Maisy, his eyes wide. "You okay, Mais?"

At the genuine concern in his tone and the sweet glow on Maisy's cheeks, I nod. "You okay, Rookie?"

"Yeah! Take a shot!" he hollers, turning back to the group.

Damien Barnes chuckles into his glass and Mila shoots Maisy and me a curious glance before accepting a shot glass.

I tug Maisy off the barstool, nudging her in front of me. My hands plant on the bar, caging her in, and keeping her safe from the drunk stumbling taking place around us.

When she's nestled against my chest, I stand straighter. At my full height, 6'2", the top of Maisy's head doesn't meet my chin. I move my arms closer together, cradling her arms in between mine.

"You want a shot?" I ask, lowering my mouth to her ear again. But this time, I've gotten control of myself. I'm not going to kiss Maisy in a crowded bar for the first time. I'm not going to set off a chain of gossip and open us up to questioning by the small town we live in.

We're not there yet. We need to take our time, tread carefully. If Asher was here, he'd smack the back of my head and tell me to go for it. But I'm the more cautious brother; the one with more to lose if a romantic connection doesn't pan out.

Maisy shakes her head, twisting her body so she can face me. "I'm ready to call it a night. I mean, if you are," she tacks on, trying to read my expression.

Shit. Dread sinks to the pit of my stomach. Did I come on too strong? Mess this up? Did I misread the signs and blow this thing with this woman before it had a chance to start?

"Sure, okay," I say easily, not wanting her to feel uncomfortable. Or worse, pressured, to hang with me. I step back, giving her room and pull my phone from my back pocket to order a car. "Uber will be here in seven minutes. I'll see you to your home."

"What about your car?"

I shake my head. "Been drinking."

She smiles. "You won't drive after one drink?"

"Gotta practice what I preach. I have a kid," I remind her, scanning through my messages. "Lola and Jas already left."

In the past, women's eyes would dim at the reminder of Lola, but Maisy's soften. "You're a good dad, Axel." Maisy reaches for me again and laces her fingers with mine.

My brow furrows as I take in our joined hands. Does she still want me to kiss her? Why can't I read the signs? I don't remember dating being this damn confusing. I feel like a fish out of water.

Maisy squeezes my hand, almost like a reassurance. But I'm supposed to give those to *her*.

Blowing out a deep breath, I settle up the bar tab, call out a farewell to the guys, and wait for Maisy to hug Mila goodbye. When she's done whispering with her friend, the two of them exchanging a series of hand gestures and widening eyes that reminds me of Lola and Jas, Maisy and I head outside to the Uber.

When Maisy slips inside, she releases my hand. I watch her the entire ride to her house, waiting for her to say something, but she remains quiet. She stares out the window, as if lost in thought. Or wanting to avoid me.

Damn, is she avoiding me?

When we pull up to her house, I ask the driver to wait a minute, so I can walk her to her front door.

"Oh, you don't have to do that," Maisy says dismissively, flicking her wrist.

"Yes, I do." I hold the door open for her. What the hell kind of man was Josh? Or the other men she dated? Jesus, is this the norm now? Will Lola date men who honk their horns instead of taking the extra three minutes to come to the door and ring the bell with some decency? I mutter under my breath about it and Maisy shoots me a questioning look. Feeling myself grow agitated, I shake my head.

Instead, I place a hand in the center of her back and escort her to her front door.

She gives me a sweet smile. "Thanks for dragging me out tonight. I had fun."

Dragging her out. Does that mean she thinks this was a friendly, team thing? Doesn't she know I think of her as more than that? Did the almost-kiss spook her? Is this her drawing a line in the sand?

I clear my throat and rock back on my heels, more confused now than I was at Corks. I stuff my hands in my pockets so I won't touch her. Reach for her. Kiss her. "Of course. I'm glad you came. It was fun."

She nods, shuffling her feet and...waiting. A breeze ripples over the porch, blowing a strand of hair into her face. She shakes her head, as if to move it, and I can't stop myself.

Slipping my hand from my pocket, I reach forward and grasp the end of the strand, pure silk, and gently tuck it behind her ear.

Her eyes bore into mine, swirling with emotions I can't read. Her gaze falls to my mouth once and I wonder if she's thinking about our almost-kiss. I wonder if she still thinks I look like Jason Momoa.

"Thanks for tonight, Axel," she says again.

I nod, unsure of what to say. "Yeah." I nearly wince at

how gruff, abrupt, I sound. "Well..." I clear my throat again. "Have a good night, Maisy."

"You too," she says.

I tip my head toward her door. "I'll wait for you to get inside." Because there's no way I'm getting back in a fucking Uber and leaving her standing on her porch, watching me drive away.

"Oh, right." She shakes her head, punching in the code for her lock.

I wait for her to open the door and flip on the light before I lift a hand in farewell. Then, I bound down the stairs and back to the Uber, feeling like a massive tool.

I look up in time to see the door close. The Uber driver pulls away from the curb and I wince.

Was that a date? A friendly exchange? A hint at a flirty arrangement?

Why can't I read the situation? Why don't I know how to do this anymore?

Jason Momoa would know what the hell to do right now.

Sighing, I pull my phone out of my pocket and feel my face burn as I read Lola's messages.

Lola: I'm home. Sorry I'm not sorry for crashing drinks at Corks.

Lola: She's great, Dad! I hope you and Maisy have fun tonight.

Lola: Ooh, no response...use protection!

Jesus, what am I going to do with my kid? Well, I guess if anyone knew how to date, or navigate dating, nowadays, it would be Lola and Jasmine, right?

Nah, they'll never let me live it down if I ask them for advice.

Blowing out a sigh, I call Asher. I'm not surprised when

I get his voicemail. He's probably scuba-diving in Mexico or hiking a glacier in Alaska. I leave him a message, asking him to call me back.

"We're here," the Uber driver says.

I look up and realize we're idling in front of my house. Sighing again, I put my phone away. Tomorrow. I'll think about this tomorrow.

"Have a good night," I mutter.

"You too," he offers.

I walk into my house and into my bedroom. But sleep never comes. I'm too busy recalling flashing blue eyes and a sweet smile.

I'm too busy worrying I don't stand a chance with Maisy Stratford at all.

———

"YOU DIDN'T KISS HER?" Lola squeals Sunday morning at breakfast.

"Shh!" I hush, my eyes darting around the cafe.

Jasmine smirks, loitering at the end of our table. Her pen hovers over her notepad as she pretends she's working. She's not. She's just hungry for gossip.

"Spill the tea," Jasmine demands.

"What?" I glance at the table. "I didn't order tea, Jas."

Lola sighs and Jasmine rolls her eyes. Giving up the facade of work, she sits down next to Lola. "We want the details. The information on what happened last night. The tea. Spill it."

I continue to look at my daughter and her friend like they've come from another planet. Sometimes, it feels like they have. Am I really that old, out of touch, at thirty-six? The guys on the team who aren't much younger than me seem to have a better pulse on how things work in today's world.

The lingo. Trendy fashion. How to fucking date.

"Tell us what happened!" Jasmine throws her hands up, her pen clattering to the floor. Even Lola looks exasperated.

Spill the tea.

"Oh," I mutter, finally getting it.

The girls stare at me. Waiting.

"I just wished her a good night," I say lamely.

Lola narrows her eyes. Jasmine wrinkles her nose. They continue to stare.

"Why the hell are you looking at me like that?" I pick up my coffee mug, feeling like a bug under a magnifying glass. In daylight. About to get burned from the inside out.

"You're clueless," Jasmine says sympathetically.

Lola shakes her head, like I'm some sad specimen to behold and not a damn defenseman in the NHL.

"I couldn't kiss her in front of the team at Corks," I say defensively.

"You're right there," Lola agrees.

"Yeah, that was smart, D," Jasmine chimes in. "But at her house?"

"Totally could have kissed her good night," Lola agrees.

"Well, I didn't," I say, my tone hard.

"Have you messaged her today? Or yesterday?" Jasmine asks.

My brow furrows, concerned. "No. Am I supposed to?"

The girls exchange a look.

"Will you see her at the arena tomorrow?" Lola asks.

"Most likely," I say, but I know I'll see Maisy. I've now created a list of reasons why I need to pass by, or through, the front office every time I enter The Honeycomb. They all have to do with getting a glimpse at her.

"Okay, then don't message. Just, talk to her at work tomorrow." Lola takes a sip of her coffee.

Jasmine nods in agreement. "But don't be weird."

"Weird?" I spit out. "How awkward do you girls think I am?"

They exchange another look.

I wave a hand and gulp my coffee. "Don't answer that."

Jasmine sighs. "My boss is giving me a look."

"Shocked," I mutter.

She snorts. "I'll see you at home, Lol. Later, D."

I wave her away and finish my coffee. It takes me a moment to realize Lola is still staring at me, her fork halfway between her plate and her mouth, suspended in air like she forgot she's eating eggs.

"What?" I groan.

She shakes her head and takes the bite of eggs. "Nothing. I just, I think Maisy could be really good for you, Dad. Don't mess this up. Just, be yourself. Be...normal."

"I am normal."

She laughs. "Friendly. Engaging. But not too desperate, you know? Like, don't stalk her."

"I'm not a stalker."

Lola rolls her eyes. "You need to find a balance. Engage with her, see her at work, but don't message her every five seconds. Or even every day. Just...act normal. It would be good for you to have someone in your life, Dad. Someone to build a future with."

I swear under my breath and nod even though I have no idea what the hell kind of advice this is. "Normal. Got it."

Lola beams.

I look around for Jasmine who suddenly, is nowhere to be found.

I need more coffee.

NINE

MAISY

"SO, you don't think it was a date?" Mila looks perplexed as she sips her vanilla latte.

I toss my hands in the air, garnering attention from the table next to us at the Coffee Grid. I flash the elderly gentleman a smile and duck my head. Turning back to Mila, I hiss, "I have no idea what to think. It's weird, right?"

"I would have staked my life on him kissing you good night."

"I mean, yeah. After he almost kissed me at Corks. It looked like he wanted to kiss me, didn't it?"

Mila gives me a look. "It looked like he wanted to lay you down and have his way with you on top of the bar."

"I wish," I grumble. Mila laughs.

"He brushed my hair out of my face," I tell her the truth.

She tilts her head, thinking. "Sweet. Sensual. So not what I pictured Brawler doing."

"I know he has a I-could-cut-off-your-wind-pipe-with-one-finger look but he really is a nice guy. A good dad."

"Yeah," Mila agrees. "Has he called?"

I groan. "That's the worst part. Nothing. I mean, I've seen him at the office—"

"And?"

"And he said hello."

Her mouth drops open. "That's it?"

I slump, this conversation making me feel worse than the downward spiral of my thoughts over the past three days. "He wished me a good day," I add miserably.

Mila's mouth drops open, and she stares at me for a full three seconds before tossing her head back and laughing.

"It's not funny, Mil!"

"You're right." She wipes the corners of her eyes, still laughing. "It's hilarious!"

I sulk, failing to see the humor in another man not being interested in me.

"I bet he doesn't know how to act around you."

"You just staked your life on him kissing me. You're dead," I remind her.

Mila sticks out her tongue and swipes up her latte, taking a long drink. "No, he's into you, Maisy. Even Damien and Beau were talking about it at Corks. I really think he doesn't know what to do with you." She leans closer, dropping her voice. "Think about it. When was his last serious relationship?"

"Years ago," I offer, recalling Axel sharing that he's been on his own—dad over everything—for years.

"And I bet he doesn't usually date women tied to his team."

"Probably not," I concede.

"And you met his daughter."

"I did," I say slowly, wondering if that threw him off. "But the almost-kiss happened *after* I met Lola."

"Yeah, but maybe it spooked him. Maybe he realizes

that things with you would be more than what he's used to. He's a big, gruff, quiet guy. The ultimate family man. Introverted, keeps to himself..." She trails off, widening her eyes.

"And?" I widen mine back, wondering where she's going with this.

"You scare him."

At this, I toss *my* head back and laugh. "I don't scare him, Mila. The guy looks like Jason Momoa."

Mila giggles. "He really does."

"Right?" I add, happy someone agrees with me. "He's hot."

"He's been single a long time."

Sighing, I pick up my coffee and take a drink. "Maybe. I just wish I could read the situation better. I hate not knowing where I stand, like I'm existing in limbo. It reminds me too much of, you know."

"Josh," my best friend says. "And Tim."

My lip curls at the mention of my ex-boyfriend and exboss. Too many men in my life who kept me walking on eggshells. Too many men in my life I *allowed* to keep me walking on eggshells.

I have an amazing dad. He's too wonderful for me to make decisions like a woman with daddy issues. But mommy issues? That's a whole other story. I guess I take after my dad in the relationship department. Like him, I'm always the pacifist, always accepting, never one to rock the boat. I've come a long way in knowing my value, in manifesting a better future, a more positive life outlook. "I'm done feeling that way. Like I don't know my own worth."

"You should be," Mila agrees. "But I don't think that's what Axel's doing."

"Me neither. I don't know what he's doing."

Mila snorts. "That's just men."

I crack a smile. "Maybe. What do you think I should do?"

"Either wait and see what happens the next time your paths cross. Or ask him out."

My mouth drops open. "Ask him out?"

"You just said you're done waiting around, feeling like you don't know where you stand. If you ask him out, you'll know. He'll either accept or turn you down and then, limbo is over."

"Jeez, Mila, do you have to take everything I say and... run with it?"

She snickers. "Hell yeah. If not me, then who? Well, besides Missy."

I roll my eyes, turning over her idea carefully in my mind. I've never asked a man out before. Hell, I never asked a boy out, not even to the Sadie Hawkins dance in high school. Or middle school. My stomach twists at the thought, at the *rejection*, that could ensue.

But what if he didn't reject me? And, why the hell should I be scared to pursue something—*someone*—I want?

I take a deep breath, recalling the wonderful professor I had in college, Dr. M. She first introduced me to yoga and then, manifestation and visualization.

You are a strong and confident woman.

Doesn't that mean being brave? Putting myself out there, fear of rejection be damned? Doesn't that mean putting myself, my wants, first sometimes?

"You could be right," I finally admit.

"Of course I'm right. How 'bout this? Give the big guy till Friday. If he doesn't make a move by then, ball's in your court."

"You know, you're getting better at using non-football analogies."

"Ah, classic avoidance." Mila shakes her head.

I shrug.

"I'm expanding my repertoire," she adds. "Trading some football lingo for other sports references."

I snort. "Devon will be disappointed that you went with basketball instead of hockey."

Mila laughs, before calmly sipping her coffee. She waits me out until I agree. Which, eventually, I always do.

"Fine," I say, but I'm unable to keep the flutter of excitement from my tone. Because as scary as the idea of asking Axel out is, it's scarier to think I'll live my life never going out on a ledge. Never going after things that make me happy. "We'll revisit this conversation on Friday."

Mila shrugs. She's such a good friend, she doesn't point out when she's right. "Or you'll already have a date."

"I hope so."

I'd love nothing more than a real date with Axel Daire. A date that ends with a good night kiss.

———

MY WISH COMES true two days later. I'm tossing my purse down on the kitchen island after finishing work when my phone rings.

When Axel Daire flashes across the screen of my Apple Watch, my heart simultaneously leaps into my throat and down to my toes.

He's calling me. He's calling me! He's calling *me.*

Calm down.

You're strong, confident, and—oh shit, where's the damn phone?

I rummage in my purse, relief skittering through my veins when my fingers wrap around the phone and pull it out of the jumble of crap my purse holds.

I draw in a deep inhale and let it out slowly, hoping my voice doesn't sound like I just went for a sprint when I answer.

To be safe, I take another deep breath. Oh crap, what if I miss the call and have to call him back?

"Hello?" I sound breathless. But breathless can be hot, right? But is this breathless sexy or breathless like I can't breathe?

"Maisy? You okay?" Axel sounds concerned and I wince. Breathless like I can't breathe.

I clear my throat. "Yes, fine. How are you?"

"Good, good," he murmurs, his voice lower than a moment ago.

"Good," I squeak, hating empty moments of silence. I plop down on a kitchen barstool and force myself to breathe, not speak.

"Yeah." He pauses. "Listen, I'm not good at this."

Two seconds tick by. This again? "At what?"

He chuckles but the sound is self-deprecating, and it eases the knot of nerves bundling in my throat. "This. I'm calling to ask you out, Maisy."

"You-you are?" Disbelief rounds out my words and I wince again.

"Yes." His voice is direct, certain. "I'd like to take you to dinner. This Friday. If you don't have plans."

The inner strong, confident, brave girl that resides in my heart goes wild, performing the latest TikTok dance with ease. As inner me shakes her money maker, outer me tries not to hyperventilate.

"I'm free."

"Good. That's good. Eight o'clock?"

"Sure." I'm breathless again.

"I'll make reservations at Le Papillon."

And I can't breathe. Because I've been dying to try the best French restaurant in Knoxville for over two years. Mila and I made plans to go once, but then Avery got a stomach bug and *needed* her.

It's not the type of place I'd feel comfortable going solo and...it's not the type of place I'd ever picture Axel at but...

I smile. He wants to take me to Le Papillon.

"Do you think you'd like that restaurant?" he asks, a hint of nerves in his voice.

My heart melts. I'm goo. A messy gush of emotion.

"I'd love that," I whisper, clenching the phone tightly.

"Good," he says, reverting to his go-to word. "I'll pick you up at eight."

I grin at the confirmation. "I'll see you then, Axel."

"Okay. 'Bye, Maisy."

I hang up the phone and squee. I let my internal girl out to get down, dancing around my kitchen like the happiest version of myself.

Axel Daire wants to take me to Le Papillon.

I call Mila.

"Hey, Mais."

"I HAVE A DATE!" I holler, shaking my ass in front of the stove.

"YEAH, GIRL!" she shouts back, always my ride or die. "When? Did he call? Text? Show up on your porch? Tell me everything."

I relocate to the living room and drop onto the sofa Axel reclaimed from Josh. The reminder makes me smile and I kick my feet up, snuggling into the plush cushions. "He called. We're going to—wait for it—Le Papillon. Friday. At eight," I rattle off the details.

"No way! That's your top to-try restaurant."

"I know!" I squeeze my eyes shut, excited and delighted and happy.

"Damn. Axel Daire knows what's up!"

"Hey!" Devon shouts in the background. "I know what the fuck is up too!"

"What are you wearing?" Mila asks, ignoring her boyfriend.

"I don't know. Can we discuss?"

"Duh. I'll be over in thirty. I'll grab Mexican for dinner," Mila says.

"Wait. What am I supposed to eat?" Devon whines.

"You'll be fine." I hear Mila kiss him. "I gotta go. It's Maisy."

"No kidding," Devon grumbles. And then, "Hey, Mais!"

"Tell Devon hi," I laugh. "See you soon."

"See you," Mila says. "I'm so excited!"

"Me too!"

When we disconnect, I lay back on my couch and turn my head to face Lux. "I got a date," I tell my fish.

She swims around, ignoring me.

"He's a hot, sexy, gruff but sweet as hell hockey player," I continue, watching Lux pop into her pirate house. "I know, I didn't see it coming either. But this is good, right? I mean, I'd been wary of Josh, and his intentions, for months before we broke up. And that was before he tried to swipe my furniture." I look around the living room, enjoying the fresh design and feel of the space. "This is a good thing."

I've got a space I feel at home in. A job I enjoy. Hobbies that fill my creative soul.

And now, a date with a man who makes my heart skip.

A date with a man who seems to revel in my curves and hang onto the words as they fall from my lips.

A man who is making my dream come true.

He's taking me to Le Papillon. I pick up a pillow and hold it to my chest, squeeing again.

And then, once more. Just because it feels good.

TEN

AXEL

I HEAVE OUT A DEEP BREATH, not sure if I look edgy and confident, like Jason Momoa (Lola got a damn kick out of that comparison). Or like a poser, trying too hard to fit in. Like, well, like how I feel.

"Stop fidgeting," Lola scolds me.

"Jason Momoa never fidgets," Jasmine adds her two cents.

I huff and grip at the collar of my shirt. It feels like I can't breathe. I yank it down several inches and pull in a large exhale.

"Stop!" Lola smacks my hand away.

"Mock turtlenecks are in, D," Jasmine reminds me.

A short-sleeved mock turtleneck. That's what I'm wearing. I've been informed by the two pipsqueaks next to me that it's *midnight* gray and a *knit* blend. It's paired with dark wash jeans and *Chelsea* boots. "I don't look like me."

"Trust, D." Jas places a hand on my shoulder. "This is the new you. It's a good look."

"Solid," my kid agrees.

I exhale and rub my hands together. I don't want to

admit it, but the material of the shirt does feel nice. It's soft and fitted but doesn't feel too snug. I could—what the hell am I thinking? It's still a damn *turtleneck.*

"You should get going." Lola passes me my wallet and phone.

"Belt or no belt?" Jasmine asks her, studying my appearance.

"No belt," I snap, swiping my stuff from Lola and stuffing it in my back pocket.

Lola wrinkles her nose. Jas shrugs. "Baby steps," I hear my daughter's bestie whisper.

Oh, brother. "Thanks for the help, girls." I need to shut this intervention down before they have me highlighting my hair and getting my eyebrows shaped. "What are you getting into tonight?"

Jasmine shoots Lola a look that I don't like. It's pointed and contains a flare of unease. Shit, are they getting into something stupid? I glance at Lola. She's giving me an easy, nonchalant smirk. I don't trust it for a second.

Lola's a good kid. She's a hard worker, gets straight As, and has a friendly disposition. But she's also a twenty-one-year-old woman in a computer science program, constantly surrounded by smart boys who didn't get laid in high school and could speak riddles around me. Algorithms. Whatever.

The point is, she's eventually going to jam herself up in some kind of situation. And I really don't want it to be tonight. I lift my eyebrows, still waiting for a damn response.

"Nothing," Lola says finally. "A dorm party. Maybe drinks at Corks."

I wince. "Corks?"

"You can't own the town bar, Dad."

"I know. But aren't there *college* bars?" When I was in college, we couldn't afford the drinks at nice sports bars.

Lola shrugs. "We may swing by for a drink or two."

I narrow my gaze. "Why?"

"Because..." Her eyes cut to Jasmine.

"We're two hardworking girls with new IDs who occasionally fancy a margarita. Or a mojito," Jas cuts in smoothly.

"You're up to something." I wag my finger between them.

"You're going to be late," Lola says again, nudging me toward the door. "We'll be fine and I'll text you when I get home tonight."

"Promise?" I pause, wondering if this is one of those moments where I should trust her judgement and give her room to make decisions without my input. Or if I should stay and find out the details of tonight's plan like I want to. Because they're going to Corks with a purpose. A purpose that could only mean meeting up with guys. And I want to know which fucking guys.

"Promise." Lola's tone is impatient.

Glancing at my watch, I groan. I am going to be late. "Be careful."

She smiles. "Love you, Dad. Have fun."

I make my way to my truck, glancing over my shoulder to make sure Lola closed the door. I have no idea what she and Jasmine are conspiring, but I need to get moving if I'm going to pick Maisy up on time.

I don't want to be late. I want Maisy to know that tonight is important to me. That this date is for real. That I don't wear turtlenecks and make dinner reservations and give a shit about being punctual. But for her, I want to.

My phone rings as I back out of the driveway and I answer via Bluetooth.

"Hey! Where the hell are you calling from?"

A chuckle sounds out. "Chile," Asher replies.

"Of course." I shake my head. "Diving?"

"Ice-hiking. But that's nothing compared to you dating."

I snort. "Lola told you?"

"Gushed is more like it." The tab of a beer can pops in the background. "Tell me about the woman in your life, brother."

"Ah, I'm actually driving to her house now. We're going out to dinner."

"Damn." My brother whistles and I can hear his smile through the line. "That's big, Axe. I'm happy for you, man. Tell me about her."

I slide my palm over the top of the steering wheel, relaxed now that I'm talking to my brother. Whenever I connect with Asher, I take a page out of his book and let my worries float away. He has that effect on people, injecting everyone around him with the cool calmness he exudes.

"Her name is Maisy. She's...well, she's the sweetest, most genuine, caring woman I've ever met in my life." The words ring true and that settles me too. Tonight, I have a date with a goddess.

———

MY MOUTH DROPS when she pulls open the door.

"You look beautiful." The words pop out of my mouth, direct with an edge of desperation because, holy shit. I try to remember everything Lola told me about being chill. Jasmine reminded me not to smother her or be overbearing. Asher advised that I play it cool, let the evening unfold naturally. They gave me rules to follow and lists to remember, but when I gaze into Maisy's clear blue eyes, I forget everything. "You are beautiful."

Her expression softens, that sweetness I love sweeping her face. "Thank you." She runs a hand over my shoulder and quirks an eyebrow. "A mock turtleneck?"

I clear my throat, my face burning. Asher choked on his beer when he learned what I was wearing tonight. "Lola."

"Ah," she laughs. "You look very nice. Sophisticated."

My ears are on fire.

Maisy takes pity on me. "I've always wanted to go to Le Papillon."

I breathe a sigh of relief. "I'm glad I could take you."

Her smile widens. "Me too."

Maisy locks up and we make our way to my truck. I help her in, my gaze zeroing in on the peach of her ass, full and juicy in a cerulean blue skirt that's gorgeous, but has nothing on the shade of her eyes. She's wearing a crisp white blouse and sexy pale peach heels. My throat dries as I envision—with perfect clarity—what those strappy sandals would look like hooked over my shoulders. Her scent, a soft floral perfume, wraps around me. I shuffle back half a step and clear my throat, trying to get my bearings.

I don't lose my head around women. I don't lose myself in women. For years, I've only given the physical aspect, sex, but never my emotions. With Maisy, I'm swimming in them and that feels exhilarating. And dangerous.

Once I close the door to my truck, I walk around the back slowly, trying to get my emotions under control. Tonight feels different but it shouldn't feel insurmountable.

"We're just getting to know each other," I remind myself. "There's no rush; we have all the time in the world."

When I slip behind the steering wheel and point the

truck toward Le Papillon, Maisy gives me the most breath-taking smile I've ever seen.

It calms my mind, soothes my nerves, and kicks my heart into overdrive.

"Have you watched *Aquaman* yet?" she asks.

I laugh, loving the surprise that flashes across her expression.

"Not yet," I admit, grinning at her.

"I like that I can make you laugh, Axel," she says, an easy smile on her face, but her eyes are serious. Intent.

"Me too, Maisy."

The drive passes quickly as Maisy and I fall into conversation. We talk about the Thunderbolts, about Mila and Devon, about the University of Tennessee.

By the time I pull up to Le Papillon and pass my keys to the valet, I'm at ease, more excited than nervous about my date.

I take Maisy's hand with confidence as we step into the restaurant and enjoy every emotion that flits across her face. Excitement, happiness, wonder, and awe.

God, she's incredible. And tonight, she's here with me.

———

"YOU HAVEN'T TAKEN a vacation in how long?" Her eyebrows nearly meet her hairline as she stares at me.

I shrug, scooping up the last bite of my mashed potatoes. "It's been a while."

"Three years is an eternity for your mental health, Axe," she blurts out, shortening my name the way my closest friends do. Not realizing she did it, she continues, "You need to recharge. Have time to relax and rest."

"You sound like Lola." No wonder they hit it off. Lola

and Maisy both lean into these concepts of wholeness that didn't hold the same weight growing up in my family. From my mom, yes, but she was the most eccentric mom of my friend group. But from my dad? Nope. He was all about paying your dues, putting in work, and hustling to obtain more. The thought of rest would have made him laugh until he cried.

"She's a smart woman," Maisy says.

"You're right," I agree, a proud papa bear.

"Okay. If you could go on vacation anywhere, where would you go?"

I take a sip of my wine and think about her question. The bold red swirls over my tongue and I try to savor the taste. I'm not much of a wine drinker but I want tonight, this date, to be perfect. Classy. I want to be a sophisticated, adult male who can order the right bottle of wine.

Maisy sighs. "Do you like the beach? Or the mountains? Being in a new city?"

I shrug. "All of them, I guess."

"You guess?" She laughs, shaking her head in disbelief. The candle in the center of our table flickers, causing the light to move over her face like a slow rolling wave. I stare, mesmerized.

"I like to fish."

Maisy rolls her lips together, as if trying to contain her laughter, as she studies me. "Of course you do."

Huh? I turn the tables. "Where would you go? Right now?"

"On a trip?"

"Yeah."

"Costa Rica."

"Seriously?" I lean closer. "How'd you answer so fast?"

Maisy blushes. "There's this surfing camp I've always wanted to go to."

"Surfing camp?" My God, sometimes it scares me how much Maisy and Lola have in common. They're both strong, smart, ambitious women with an adventure-seeking side. Maisy would hit it off with Asher too. The thought makes me grin. "You surf?"

"Not yet."

I snort. "And you're just going to go to Costa Rica and learn?"

"Exactly."

I shake my head, trying to piece this together. "This sounds like a scheme Lol and Jas would try to get me to sign off on for spring break."

Maisy laughs again.

"Walk me through this." I stare at Maisy, wanting to understand her better. All of her.

"I saw this camp, it's like a retreat—yoga, surfing, living on a beach—on television years ago. I was a UT student at the time, must have been my sophomore year. I wrote it down in my goal journal."

"Your what?" I cough on my wine.

"Goal journal," she repeats, expression serious. And then, "You don't have a goal journal?"

"What do you think?"

"That's what I'm getting you for Christmas."

The joke, so freely given, makes my heart beat faster. Does she see us together by Christmas? Can she envision us exchanging presents, decorating a tree, *celebrating* together?

The thought pulls me up short. Since my parents passed, both of them within a year of each other, I always spend Christmas with Lola, Anna and Ben, and their boys in Seattle. If Asher isn't off on an adventure, he joins us, but it's always a last-minute thing. I can't start messing with traditions, with holidays, can I?

"Axe?" Maisy frowns and I realize she asked me a question.

"Huh?" I shake my head to clear it.

A moment of wariness flickers in her eyes before she smiles past it. "I asked what you're doing this weekend."

"Oh," I say, mentally running through my weekend plans. Tomorrow, I'm volunteering at the Children's Hospital. I do it one Saturday of the month, goofing off, playing games, with some of the kids. It's something I started when I was a freshman in college and I've carried it with me through every move and team transition. Sunday, I have my standing brunch with Lola. "Not much."

"No plans at all?" Maisy tilts her head to the side. "If you're free tomorrow afternoon—"

"No," I cut her off. I have to be at the hospital at noon. "I'm not free until later on in the day."

"Oh," she says, and again, I note the hesitancy in her gaze.

Frowning, I ask. "Why?"

She spears a mushroom with her fork. "No reason. Forget it. What else is going on?"

"Not much. Just hockey."

"Do you have any big games coming up?"

"We're playing Miami next week. Then, Chicago. We play Boston next month. The Hawks are tough as hell to go up against. I wonder if it will be strange for Scotch, considering he used to play for them." I reference our Coach and part-owner of the Thunderbolts.

"I hadn't thought of that. It will be an intense game?"

I roll my lips together, amused by how little she knows about hockey. Not that I've dated much, but the women I did mess around with were always fans of the game. "It will be a good experience for the Bolts to go up against tough competition. The Hawks are a solid team."

"Right," she says, nodding.

I wrack my head for something smart, something inquisitive to ask her but come up empty. Why is this so difficult? I've wanted to take Maisy on a date since the moment I laid eyes on her, months ago, but she was in a relationship and off-limits. Now, we're seated in a romantic French restaurant, and the only thing I can think to talk about is...work?

Inwardly, I groan and pick up my wine glass, draining it.

ELEVEN

MAISY

IS HE NERVOUS? Bored? Ready to leave?

Axel Daire is a difficult man to read on a good day. Tonight, he's impossible. Other than the blatant appreciation in his eyes when he picked me up, I've barely gotten a smile, a reaction, out of him all night.

The man doesn't vacation, doesn't willingly share his weekend plans, and, as far as I can tell, his only hobby is fishing. He's spoken about Lola and the Thunderbolts all night. And only because I've peppered him with questions.

I take a generous sip of my wine. It's not a bad date. Not at all. It's just...not the fireworks I expected. Narrowing my gaze, I zero in on Axel's mock turtleneck and slicked back hair. His long hair is secured at the nape of his neck, a neat man bun when I'm used to seeing it messy and in disarray. He clearly tried to look a certain way tonight but...

Oh God, is he disappointed in me? Does he find me lacking? This date, conversation, inadequate?

My mother's voice, words from my teen years, ping through my head. *Sit up straight. Push your shoulders back.*

You'll never land a man if you slouch. Be interesting but not too chatty; never too much.

Or do I need to manage my own expectations? The conversation has been pleasant enough, the food, delicious. There's nothing bad or wrong and yet, my chest squeezes. A part of me is disappointed because I was expecting...more. Something big and overwhelming, imposing, like Axel.

"Do you like to fish?" he asks after a long pause, circling back to his one hobby.

"I've never been."

"Ever?"

I shake my head, giving a small smile and a cute shrug. At least, I hope it's cute. Maybe he'll offer to take me? Maybe he'll want to teach me how to fish. Maybe—

"That's too bad," he says.

Maybe not.

"Do you fish a lot?" I wade back in.

Axel shrugs, his mouth almost curling into a smile at a faraway thought, maybe a memory, before smoothing out in a straight line. Can he just give me one smile? A hint that shows he wants to be here with *me*? That this isn't deficient or awful?

"I used to go more in Seattle."

"Would you like to see a dessert menu?" Our server pops by and begins to clear our plates.

Axel looks at me expectantly.

I love dessert. I always save room for a sweet treat at the end of the meal. The dessert menu here boasts macarons and mille-feuille, lemon tarts and opera cake.

My stomach is tied in knots. The thought of biting into a perfectly sour tart and enduring any more of this stifled conversation, unable to read the insanely sexy man seated across from me, makes my eyes burn.

"No, thank you," I murmur.

Axel frowns, his expression tightening. "You sure?"

Does he think I can't pass up a dessert? Or is finally clueing into the stilted conversation, hesitant and stumbling, between us?

"I'm sure."

"I'm fine, too," he tells our server.

"All right." She places down the black bill book. "I'll leave this for whenever you're ready. No rush."

Axel reaches for it moments after she leaves the side of our table and my heart sinks into the clustered knots of my stomach. I make a move to grab my purse and he gives me a sharp look, his dark eyes black with intensity. "Thank you for coming with me, Maisy." His tone is stern and I place my hands back in my lap.

"Thank you for dinner, Axel." So formal.

He nods, slipping his credit card into the black folder.

I clear my throat. "What's Lola doing tonight?"

He sighs. "I'm not sure but she and Jas are getting into something."

"Really? What do you think?"

He snorts, the most amused he's been all evening. "That's the problem. I don't know. They were being cryptic as hell. But they're going to Corks which means—"

"They're going to see some guys."

"Exactly." Axel frowns, as if my confirming it made it true. He sighs, thanking the server when she runs his card. He adds a tip and signs his name, tucking the slip of paper into the little book. "You ready?"

I nod, standing from my chair and tucking it back under the table. Disappointment squeezes my throat like a vice, making speech impossible.

"Maisy?" My name rings out.

Turning, I spot Cohen, one of the football players for the Knoxville Coyotes and my longtime friend. Relief eases my disappointment and I relax when I catch his eyes. Bright green and brimming with humor.

"Cohen! What are you doing here?" I blush the moment the words are out of my mouth, noticing the beautiful redhead behind him. I lift my hand in a little wave and she smiles.

"On a date," he quips, reaching my side. He palms my waist, leaning in to kiss my cheek. "You?" His eyebrow arches.

I clear my throat, my blush deepening. "Same."

Cohen nods and holds out a hand to Axel. "Good to see you, man."

"You too," Axel mutters, gruff as always. He shakes Cohen's hand, but his expression is harder than it was a moment ago. Unreadable as always.

Cohen grins and shoots me a wink. "Have a good night, Maisy. I'll catch up with you this week."

"Of course," I agree, squeezing his forearm. "See you soon."

As Cohen and his date, a gorgeous woman whose laughter ripples through the space like a melody, step past us on their way to the bar, I can't help but watch. Cohen is charming, affable, likable, and fun to be around. His date hasn't stopped smiling up at him, her eyes filled with a mixture of awe and desire.

"You know him well?" Axel's voice slices through my thoughts and I turn my attention back to my date.

"We've been friends for years." Cohen used to be best friends with Mila's ex-boyfriend Avery Callaway. Cohen and Mila were extremely close, like brother and sister. After Avery's cheating scandal became public, their friendship, and subsequently, my friendship with Cohen, took a hit. But now, they've reconciled and it's nice to see my old friend again.

I look over my shoulder one last time and catch his eye. Cohen's staring straight at me, his expression searching, gaze sharp, as he takes in Axel's hand on the small of my back, guiding me forward. Huh? Does he not like Axel? There's been some rivalry between the Coyotes and the Bolts since the new team arrived early in summer, but Cohen isn't one for drama.

His date laughs again, drawing his attention back to her expectant face. He gives her an easy smile, his demeanor relaxing. Already, their body language is more in sync than mine and Axel's have been the entire night.

I allow Axel to guide me forward and search for something to fill the silence between us. We step outside, into the cool night breeze, and wait for his truck.

I let out a slow exhale and try to change the direction of my thoughts. I do what I do best: rationalize. My expectations were too high. My attraction for Axel too great. There was nothing bad about tonight. It was a perfectly pleasant meal and conversation.

But why didn't he smile and laugh? Or tease and prod? Where are the sparks I've come to associate with him? The sparks Cohen effortlessly gave off with a date, probably a random woman he's known for a handful of hours. How come their connection seemed more effortless than mine and Axel's?

I don't want perfectly pleasant. I don't want to settle for anything less than all. I want consuming intensity that threatens to drown me. I want sexy looks and hot hands, desperate caresses and intentional conversation. I want verbal foreplay.

I curse my expectations for tonight.

I slide into the passenger seat of Axel's truck. We listen to a country station on the ride home, both of us lost to our thoughts. As the city lights fade and my hometown slips past the window, I can't help feeling defeated.

I'm still here, still trying to make the most of each day. Still alone. Cohen meets and dates women regularly, each one a fun and exciting encounter that seems easy. Uncomplicated.

Mila and Devon, an unlikely pair, are in love and making plans for the future. Even my little sister, Missy, is getting serious with her boyfriend Brennan.

I've always wanted that. Marriage, a home, a family. But as my prospects dwindled and my choices in men became less reliable, I began to search for other wants. Travel, adventure, learning new things.

Is it wrong to want both? To harbor secret desires and wants, wishes and dreams? I swore to myself after Josh that I was done settling. I'm ready to live.

To surf in Costa Rica. To pursue my passions—crafting and design—with abandon. To date men who make me feel like I'm drowning and burning and needing.

I thought tonight was the start of that, but when Axel pulls into my driveway and slips from his seat, leaving the truck running, I can't fight the hurt that anchors in the pit of my stomach.

He walks me to my front door, his gaze watchful, his expression wary.

"I had fun tonight, Maisy." His tone is filled with honesty.

I turn toward him on my front porch and force a smile. "Me too. Thanks for taking me to Le Papillon."

"Anytime," he murmurs, and I can tell he means it.

That's what's so damn confusing. I can't read the man before me and I'm desperate to understand him. What is this between us? Nervous energy and awkward silence mixed with moments of anticipation? It's confusing.

Axel stares right at me, his eyes momentarily unguarded. And I see it—the spark, the hesitancy, the confusion. It's the same feelings swirling around my chest. Silent questions and sad assumptions.

Axel moves closer and my heart hammers. I tip my face up, my eyes searching his. He bends and his mouth brushes over mine in a chaste, sweet kiss. His lips are softer than they have any right to be. They move over my mouth in a slow, measured moment. The heat of his big hand seeps into my waist and the scruff of his beard tickles my chin. He kisses me again. "Thank you for tonight, Maisy."

"I, you're welcome," I manage. It's not often I'm caught off guard, but right now, I'm useless. All I can do is watch as Axel bounds down the porch steps.

He turns, walking backwards, and shoots me a grin. A real smile that curves his mouth and makes his eyes dance. It strikes me like Cupid's arrow and I smile back, wide and warm. The tightness in my chest unravels and for a heartbeat, it feels like my feet don't touch the ground.

"Go inside now," he murmurs.

Rolling my eyes at his overprotectiveness, I acquiesce, unlocking my door and slipping over the threshold.

I give him a flirtatious smirk and wave goodbye. He beeps his truck horn once before backing out of my driveway.

Closing my front door, I press my back against it and sink down to the floor. I'm more confused than ever. After a night of dancing around topics and never fully settling on one, of never digging past the surface, Axel kissed me good night. A gentle, sweet kiss that hinted at what lies beneath the surface.

A surface I'm desperate to crack. I want to explore more with him. I want to get to know the man behind the guarded eyes and hesitant smiles.

Was tonight a first step? A hint? Will he give me more or allow his guard to slip back into place?

I press my fingertips against my lips, still warm from the pressure of his.

Tonight wasn't fireworks but it was sparks. Enough to fill my empty chest with a hope that has the potential to burn into something brighter.

———

MY HOPE HAS DEFLATED.

"He still hasn't called?" Mila throws a hand in the air, exasperated.

"I read into things," I decide, leaning back in my chair at the Coffee Grid.

"No, you didn't." Mila swipes up a scone and bites into it, chewing loudly. "I don't get him. Devon says I shouldn't try. Brawler's a mystery."

"Yeah," I agree. That doesn't mean I want to solve his riddles any less. It doesn't mean I'm not more intrigued, desperately curious, to better understand the slivers of him that he shows me. Never fully enough, never all at once. Only in shades that keep me moving closer, drawn like a moth to a flame.

"I don't know, Mais. But a good night kiss is promising."

"It was practically a peck," I remind her. "Does that even count?"

She shrugs but her lack of a verbal answer means no, it doesn't.

It's been two days since my date with Axel and still, no word. I didn't see him at work this morning, which was unusual.

Is he avoiding me? Does he wish he never asked me out? Is he disappointed by how our date ended?

Stop, I mentally berate myself. *You are strong and confident. You had a first date with a good man. No need to overthink it.*

"You're overanalyzing this," Mila points out gently.

"Wouldn't you?"

She nods, looking as miserable as I feel.

"What do you think I should do?"

Mila huffs out a breath. "I think you should confront him."

"What?" I panic at the thought, scratch that, the word *confrontation.* "I don't do that," I remind my best friend. For years, my sister encouraged me to speak up for myself with our mom. To tell her how hurtful her words and comparisons are. I've never been able to do it and since then, I've rarely been able to stand up for myself at all.

"I don't mean a showdown. I think you should ask him. Just be upfront and real with him. He's tossing you mixed signals and confusing the hell out of you. How do you feel right now?"

"Confused," I admit.

"Exactly. Aren't you tired of feeling that way?"

I think back to my relationship with Josh. I'm not a doormat and I'm done being walked on, or over. "Yes."

"So, just ask him what's up. Tell him you had a great time at dinner and thought he would have called. Ask him if he wants to do something—maybe grab a coffee? Just talk to him, Maisy."

I let out an exhale that sounds like a hiss. "I'm already breaking out in hives," I admit.

Mila chortles. "It's not that bad. You need to stand up for yourself. If Axel isn't willingly giving you any signs to go off of, then you need to seek them out on your own. Why shouldn't you? You deserve to know where you stand, what he's thinking. He can't just keep giving you hope and then avoiding you."

"You're right," I agree, thinking back to the last time we did this, just a few weeks ago. "I'll...talk to him," I force out the words.

Mila smiles and holds up her coffee mug for cheers. I clink mine against it, feeling less celebratory than my bestie.

"I'm not looking forward to this," I remind her.

"I know. But you're strong and confident, Maisy."

I roll my eyes. "I regret telling you any of my daily affirmations and manifestations."

"Don't." She sips her coffee, eyes dancing. "I'm only giving you this little nudge because you're ready. Josh and Tim held you back for years. Don't let any man, any person, have control over your emotions, your worth, like that. You deserve some clarification from Axel. Go get it."

"I will," I say, an edge to my tone that wasn't there before. "You're right."

"Usually am." Mila dusts her shoulder off and I groan.

Then, we both break into laughter, and I grin at my best friend. Even though she's pushing me outside my comfort zone, she's right. I deserve more, better.

And I'm going to take it.

TWELVE
AXEL

THE BAR RATTLES against the weight rack as I drop it back in place. Sitting up on the bench, I wipe a towel across my forehead. I glance around the weight room, noting the other guys on my team.

Devon's doing shrugs, his eyes trained on his traps in the mirror. Beau Turner is chuckling at something Damien Barnes said. The two of them, easygoing and affable, remind me of Cohen. I frown, taking in the way Beau grins without a second thought, how Damien cracks jokes like he can't *not* find amusement in something as dull as weightlifting.

Shit. I take a swig of water. Did I mess everything up with Maisy?

Our date wasn't bad. It just wasn't what I wanted it to be. I wanted perfection. I mean I wore a mock freaking turtleneck and drank wine and ate fancy French food. I thought that would count for something. Instead, I said good night to Maisy feeling even more unsettled than when I picked her up hours earlier.

Sighing, I drop back to the bench and grip the bar, doing another set of bench presses. My knuckles pop and sweat drips down my forearms as I continue to lift, wanting to work the aggravation and disappointment I feel out of my system.

"Hey, man," Devon greets me when I finish my next set.

I nod in his direction, guzzling water instead of responding.

"Have a good weekend?" His tone is too innocent.

"It was fine."

He arches a perfectly shaped blond eyebrow.

I groan. "What'd Mila say?"

"That you haven't called Maisy yet." He responds so quickly that I chortle. Innocent and casual my ass. "Date not go well?"

Fucking hell. This is why I don't date. This is why I don't rush things. When you rush into them, there are expectations and labels and gossip. Three things I can't stand.

"It was fine." My tone is clipped and Devon grins.

"Look, I'm the last guy who should pass out relationship advice—"

I nod in agreement. Just a few months ago, Devon nearly burned what he was building with Mila to the ground.

"But if you like her, call her. Sooner rather than later." He gives me a pointed look before moving toward Barnes and Turner. The three of them laugh at another one of Barnes's wisecracks.

Would Maisy be better off with a guy like one of them? Well, not Devon, but Barnes or Turner? A man like Cohen?

I growl as the thought circles in my head again. It's been on a loop since I saw that sunshine smile she gave him at Le Papillon. It doesn't matter that he was on a date with a fiery redhead. The way he looked at Maisy, the concern he held for her, speaks to a history.

My stomach churns. I'm not jealous. I just...I want a real shot with Maisy Stratford, and I've got no clue how the hell to do that without coming on too strong. She just got out of an awful working environment and a shitty relationship. I don't want to be her rebound. But I sure as hell don't want to be the guy standing on the sidelines, watching men like Cohen, or Barnes, or hell, like Asher—why can't I be more like my brother?—schmooze her either.

Jesus, what is wrong with me?

Biting back a swear, I do another set for the hell of it. When I leave the weight room, I don't feel any less pissed off than before my workout. But I do consider Devon's advice.

Call her. Sooner rather than later.

———

THE SENTIMENT IS ECHOED LATER that night when I have dinner with Lola and Jasmine.

"You haven't called her yet?" My daughter glares at me.

"What's wrong with you, D?" Jas shakes her head.

"I didn't want to smother her," I say, defensive. So defensive, I shove a handful of French fries into my mouth, effectively destroying the extra sets I performed at the gym this morning.

"She's probably confused," Lola advises. "Especially if the date didn't go well."

"It didn't go badly," I counter.

Asher's text—*how'd your date go?*—circles through my mind, calling me a liar. If the date was awesome, I would have messaged him back.

Jasmine gives me a sympathetic look that has me reaching for her fries.

It did go badly. It wasn't what I expected. It wasn't what I wanted for her. For us. Recalling the disappointment in her gaze, the way her expression flattened after each question she asked was met with my usual taciturn response, makes my chest feel funny. I let her down.

But God she looked so gorgeous. And the collar on my shirt was so damn tight. And I didn't know which wine to order, or which fork to use or how to do anything right. Not like Cohen, who waltzed in and had every woman in the damn place beaming at him.

"Call her," Jasmine advises, pulling the fries out of my grasp.

"Better yet, ask her out again. To do something fun, not frilly," Lola adds. "What does she like to do?"

I furrow my eyebrows, thinking.

"Like, for a hobby," Jasmine says slowly, spelling it out.

"I know what you mean," I snap. Hobby. Didn't Maisy ask me that? Am I the only person who doesn't have hobbies I do regularly? "She likes art. Crafting. That kind of thing."

Lola and Jasmine stare at me like I'm hopeless. Maybe I am. Maybe it's not supposed to be this hard and I'm not cut out for it, dating, anymore. Maybe I should back off and—

"She mentioned that at Corks," Jasmine says, looking at Lola.

"I got it!" Lola snaps her fingers. "Wine and paint."

"Ooohhh," Jasmine squeals. "That's a great idea. You'll love this place, D."

"Doubt it." I sulk, since I rarely love anything with the same enthusiasm as the two pipsqueaks devouring all the French fries.

"You will," Lola determines, unaffected by my tone.

"There's an art studio, not too far from campus, that started a series of wine and paint nights. They have classes focused on nature, abstract, portrait. They have theme nights and different charcuterie boards to pair with the wine. It's super cute."

"Totally date night appropriate." Jasmine nods along with Lola.

I heave out a sigh. "Wine and paint." I'm not the kind of man that wines and paints but—

"She'll love it," Lola decides.

"And you owe her a better date," Jasmine reminds me.

"I'll look into it," I say, noncommittally. By the satisfied smirks on both girls' faces, they know I'm lying. I'm going to book it. Because they have a better pulse on what a woman would want to do on a date than I do. Because I need all the advice I can get.

Whether I take it or not is up to me but that night, after dinner plates are cleared away and Lola texts me that she and Jasmine are back on campus, I click on the link she texted me.

An entire world—an artistic world—opens up on screen. Mom would have loved this and thinking of my mom, of Mom and Maisy meeting, makes me smile. They would have hit it off. As I check out the class offerings, everything from formal instruction to casual wine and paint, I'm impressed. I see what Lola and Jasmine meant. Hell, I understand what Maisy was hinting at with hobbies. I need one. An outlet. Something other than fishing, which I don't do regularly enough.

I crack open a beer and take a deep pull. Then, I sign Maisy and me up for a wine and paint class. Now, I just need to convince her to attend. I need to make it up to her and show her that even though I have no clue what the future holds, we have something worth exploring in the now. I haven't liked a woman, felt a pull toward anyone of the opposite sex, for years. Now that I have, I can't waste it. Not without giving it a chance.

But will Maisy want to give me another chance? Will she say yes to wine and paint?

———

I DON'T HAVE to wait long for my answer.

The following day, at The Honeycomb, Ms. Maisy Stratford marches up to me and squares her shoulders. "We should talk."

Her tone, decisive, confident, and serious, gives me pause but also makes me want to smile. Because she's unwavering and so goddamn beautiful.

"Okay," I agree, following her into an empty conference room located near the front office.

She closes the door behind us, her eyes darting around the space before settling on my face. Maisy crosses her arms over her tangerine sundress, pushing up the sleeves on her white cardigan in the process. She bites her bottom lip uncertainly and I feel like a jackass for mucking up our date so badly.

"I'm sorry," I blurt out before she can start.

Surprise flares in her irises. "For what?"

"Our date. I was nervous," I admit.

"You were?"

A slow chuckle rumbles through my chest. "Didn't you notice? I didn't know what to say, what to order. Hell, I could barely breathe in that stupid sweater."

"Mock turtlenecks look good on you," she murmurs, a hint of amusement in her eyes.

"I wanted it to be perfect."

"Me too," she whispers. "And I was nervous. I, I feel a lot for you, Axel. Considering we hardly know each other, you affect me."

"I haven't dated anyone in a long time, Maisy. Each step is a stumbling block for me. I know I should have called, but I didn't know what to say." I sigh, "Our first date wasn't great—"

"It wasn't awful." Realizing what she said, her eyes widen, her mouth dropping into an O.

But her honesty, so real and refreshing, causes me to smirk. "I can do better."

She laughs and shuffles closer to me. "I think we can both do better. My last relationship—" She pauses, pursing her lips as she chooses her words.

Fucking Josh.

"Always made me feel like I was walking on eggshells. I don't like feeling insecure."

"You have nothing to feel insecure about," I tell her truthfully, moving closer to her. It's as if I'm drawn, unable to stop myself from reaching up and brushing her honey-colored hair over her shoulder, my fingertips brushing the soft material of her sweater.

"You're difficult to read," she admits, watching me closely for a reaction to her words.

"I know," I admit. "But I don't want to be that way with you." I clear my throat, stuffing a hand in my pocket. "I haven't stopped thinking about you."

"Really?" Her voice is hushed and something about it scrapes at the walls of my chest.

"Really."

She lets out a slow breath. "I don't want to date

someone and feel like I'm always on the outside. I already did that and...it wasn't great."

I take a second to absorb her words, to understand what she's truly saying. We don't have a shot, at anything, if we can't communicate. And fuck, communication is tough for me. It's something I've been told countless times, mostly by Lola's mom when we were still dating, and then afterwards, as we navigated co-parenting. It became easier when she married Ben and our friendship solidified, but the same issues plagued me in my last serious relationship. And with my teammates on the Rams and here. "I keep things close to the chest," I try to explain. "For a long time, Lola, and my brother Asher, have been the people I talk to. But I obviously can't talk to my daughter about everything."

"You have a brother?" Maisy asks.

I snort, rolling my lips together as I nod. "Point taken."

She softens, a small smile flitting over her mouth. "Older or younger?"

"Younger by three years. He's a free spirit, roaming around the world seeking adventures."

Her brow furrows, almost like she doesn't believe me.

"You'd love him," I admit, not adding that he'd adore her too. They're very similar. I reach for her, brushing my hand over her arm. "Can we try again? I want to take you somewhere."

Maisy stares at me for a long beat, her eyes searching. "Okay," she agrees.

Surprised by her quick response, I backtrack. "Don't you want to know where we're going?" I'd hate not knowing, not having any control over the plan.

She shakes her head. "No. I like surprises. Spontaneity. I want to trust you, Axel."

Her words infuse my stomach with a warmth I haven't

felt in years. I want to be the man she trusts. I don't want to disappoint her. I want to be a man, the man, who builds her up. "Wear old clothes."

She frowns.

"It's going to get messy. Maybe," I tack on, confusing her further.

As her nose bunches and her brow furrows, I grin. Maisy Stratford is adorable and sweet. She's authentic and real. She's giving me another chance to prove that there's something between us. That there could be *more*, if we allow it.

"I'll pick you up tomorrow. At six." I squeeze her forearm.

"I'll be ready," she agrees.

I move to walk past her, but her hand darts out, stopping me. I pause, inhaling her sweet floral perfume, and turn to look at her.

Her blue eyes, bright and deep, hold me captive. "Thank you, Axel."

I shake my head. "Just give me a shot, Mais. And don't ever feel like you can't talk to me. I know I don't make it easy, but I want to know everything you're willing to share."

"Okay," she murmurs.

"See you tomorrow?"

"At six," she confirms.

I head to the ice after that, grateful for the skate. With my mind finally at rest, and my frustration quelled, I focus on practice.

And then, I go home and think about my date with Maisy.

THIRTEEN

MAISY

I'M ROCKING ripped jeans and a casual black shirt, throwback Nikes, and a belt bag. My hair is pulled back in a messy bun. My makeup is subtle. I am the most under-dressed and understated I've ever been for a date, and it feels right.

More right than anything I shared with Josh. And better than the nerves that pinged around my stomach when Axel took me to Le Papillon.

Tonight, my expectations are managed. But my excite-ment, for the surprise, for the laidback vibe, for getting to see more of the real Axel, surges.

He knocks on the front door a little before six. When I pull it open, his eyes fill with appreciation. "You look perfect."

"I don't know about that," I laugh. "But I'm excited to learn more about this surprise."

"I'm not giving anything away," he swears. "You really like surprises?"

I nod. "You don't?"

"Can't stand them. I like to plan."

"I can see that. You're very...intentional."

"How diplomatic."

I laugh. "How would you describe yourself?"

He ponders this while I step out onto the porch and lock up. "Serious," he says finally.

"Nothing wrong with that."

"Lola thinks I need to have more fun. She's always telling me not to overthink things. To live in the moment. My brother backs her up, so it's two against one."

"You disagree?"

His frown deepens. "I don't know," he says when we reach his truck. He pulls open the passenger door for me. "I guess...I guess I never had the chance to live in the moment. Lola was born when I was sixteen and after that there was always expectations. There needed to be a plan." His voice is low, lined with his usual gruffness, but I can tell he's trying to open up. His body is angled toward mine, his hands gesturing as he speaks.

"That makes sense," I say, understanding things through his worldview. Living in the moment is a luxury, one for people who don't have to provide for dependents. "I never thought about how that perspective would change with having children. Especially so young."

"I've never known anything else. It's made me..."

"Serious."

A small smile turns his lips. "Serious."

"Well, tonight we're being spontaneous."

His smile grows, giving me a glimpse of how beautiful he is when not scowling. "Because of you," he admits. Crossing his arms, he leans against the open passenger door. "Since our dinner, I realized I don't have any hobbies."

I snort out a laugh. "Do you want some?"

"I'm considering it. I'll let you know after tonight."

At his cryptic response, my curiosity spikes. "And you're not going to give me any hints?"

"And ruin the surprise you say you love? No way. Buckle up," he says, before shutting the passenger door and rounding the truck.

While Axel drives closer to the UT campus, I wrack my mind for ideas. I search outside for clues. I pepper him with questions.

But he doesn't budge, just gives me pointed looks and vague replies. His specialty.

When we pull up to a small art-studio/bistro, my excitement ticks up. "Oh my God! We're painting!"

"We are," Axel confirms.

"Do you like to paint?" I turn toward him. "Because of your mom?"

"I haven't painted since I was a kid. With Mom, yes. We always did fun, messy projects. Even when Lola was a kid, Mom would encourage finger-painting. She'd hang paper on the windows and let Lol go to town. But now," he exhales, "I guess we'll find out." He turns off his truck and slips from the driver's seat.

My heart melts. This man. This big, overpowering, intentional, purposeful, serious man is stepping so far out of his comfort zone right now to do something special for me. Me. A woman he's taking on a second date and trying to prove—what? That we really do have a connection?

The significance of tonight takes on new meaning and already, I know it's going to be better than our fancy dinner. It's going to be more meaningful than anything I shared with Josh. Or Mitch, my ex before Josh. Or Keith, my ex before Mitch.

Tonight, is a turning point in my romantic life. It's going to make or break the connection I have with Axel. Tonight is as intentional and purposeful as the man waiting for me to slide out of his truck.

I hop down, liking the way Axel catches my elbow to steady me. His hand, big and strong and reliable, slides down to my wrist and squeezes once before releasing me.

We enter the art studio, welcomed by the delicious aroma of food, before the scent of acrylic paint greets us. Axel glances around, taking in the bar, the small restaurant occupying one side, and then, the studio. The works of art that hang on the walls and line the shelves. The corridor of workspaces, places to paint and sculpt and create. Spaces that encourage the freedom to get messy.

"Welcome to the Art Attic," a woman dressed in a royal blue caftan greets us.

"Thanks," Axel says gruffly, pulling out his phone to pull up the information for the class we're taking.

"Ah," the woman says softly, a spark lighting her eyes. "It's just this way. I'm Mel."

"Axel," Axel says.

"Hi!" I wave. "I'm Maisy."

Mel smiles. "It's nice to meet you both. Would you like some wine? Perhaps something to eat?"

Axel and I exchange a look. Should we eat here? Does he want to have dinner afterwards? Are we drinking?

"Are you hungry?" Axel asks.

I shrug, not wanting to say, "I can always eat." But I can always eat.

"How about a charcuterie board and two glasses of wine—"

"Merlot," I toss out helpfully.

"Merlot," Axel agrees, his posture relaxing. "And then, we can always add on more afterwards."

"Certainly," Mel says easily. "I'll settle you into your workspace and put in your order. Follow me."

Axel and I fall into step behind Mel, and I can't help but note how his eyes peer into each workspace we pass, curious and a little confused. Is he thinking about his mom? Did she used to paint in a space like this? Does being here bring back memories?

I grip his hand and squeeze his fingers. "We're going to have fun tonight, Axe," I murmur, shortening his name the way he's shortened mine.

His dark eyes find mine, earnest. "I already am, Mais."

I bite my bottom lip and duck my head as Mel leads us into the room our class is taking place. She helps us set up with the necessary paints and brushes. Axel and I sit down in front of two canvases and introduce ourselves to some of the other participants, making small talk, until our wine and snacks arrive.

We've just sipped our wine when our teacher enters the room, clapping his hands together. "*Bonsoir, mes amis.*" He sweeps his arms to the sides wildly. "My name is Francois. I will be leading tonight's class on portrait painting. Woo!" Francois fans himself. "Wait until you meet our model. He is *très* sex-xy," he emphasizes the words.

I snort, unable to hold back my laughter as Axel's eyes bulge. Panic crosses his face and it's the sweetest, most hilarious expression I've seen him sport.

Pam, the grandmother of nine, across from us, whistles appreciatively.

My laughter ricochets around the room, increasing in volume when I take in poor Axel's haunted expression.

"Let's give Benoit a welcoming applause!" Francois announces.

Pam bolts up from her chair, her cane clattering to the

ground, as she claps enthusiastically. A few other members of our class join her, and I grip my side as my laughter, my fascination with this moment, grips me.

Benoit enters the room, wearing a poofy white shirt and trousers. His hair is slicked back from his face, tied at the nape of his neck with a navy ribbon. And he's brandishing a...sword. A real gold one, that seems a natural extension of his hand. And a *package* that has Pam's eyes widening, her hand clutching her proverbial pearls.

Dead. I'm dead.

"What did you sign us up for?" I manage to sputter out.

Axel turns toward me, his expression frozen in shock. Highlighted in horror.

My laughter bubbles upward again and I'm silently shaking with it. My eyes are tearing.

"Welcome to the romanticism of the eighteenth century!" Francois continues, helping Benoit to the center of the room, where a small, circular stage sits.

"He's wearing a poet shirt," I comment to no one. "With bishop sleeves."

In my peripheral vision, Axel's head swings toward mine. "How do you know that?"

I shrug, wiping away my tears of mirth. I look at him, smiling so wide my cheeks ache. "This is the best date I've ever been on."

At the genuine happiness he reads in my face, he relaxes, releasing a chuckle. "I booked the wrong class."

"This is genius."

"It's a mistake."

"I'm so excited."

Axel dips his head, his cheeks pinking. Oh my God, is he blushing? "I'm glad."

"Axel," I say, waiting for his eyes to latch onto mine

before continuing. "We're going to have fun tonight," I remind him.

"I already am, Mais." He gives me the same answer, which eases some of my nerves over his obvious panic.

"Me too."

"Now, let us take out our first brush," Francois says, demanding our attention. "And pay particular attention to the curves of Benoit's muscles. The tightness of his abdomen."

Axel groans next to me.

"The impressive size of...well, Benoit."

"Amen," Pam murmurs, gulping her wine.

"The strength and vibrancy, the nostalgia and longing, should be evident in your masterpieces this evening." Francois walks around the space, giving bits of encouragement to the participants.

The group begins to paint.

I roll my lips together as Axel grumbles, pulling out a paintbrush and heaving a long sigh.

"I'm going to disown Lola," he mutters.

My laughter seeps out. At the sound, Axel swears, but the sound is cheerful. In the next moment, the two of us are laughing together.

Axel's face, open and overcome with mirth, is the most beautiful I've ever seen him. He tosses his head back, his jaw on full display, his beard quivering with the waves of laughter that bubble up from his chest. His eyebrows, dark slashes, are raised with amusement. And his eyes, always so heavy, black like midnight, are colored charcoal, more hypnotizing than a fire.

"I'm sorry, Mais," he wheezes out.

I shake my head. "You're beautiful, Axe."

The observation tumbles from my mouth like a confession. Since it's the truth, I don't regret saying it.

Axel's laughter dies in his throat and his eyes turn solemn, serious, once more. "And you're exquisite, Maisy. Already, you've opened my mind and..." He works a thick swallow, his Adam's apple bobbing. "You're changing things for me."

I reach out and link our hands together. "It's the same for me. Now, let's paint."

"You still want to do this?" he asks, tipping his head hopefully.

"Hell yeah," I say, my eyes darting to Francois and Benoit. "I'd pay good money to do it again."

Axel groans but he dips his paintbrush in a tan-tinted paint and begins to roughly outline Benoit's shape.

Not gonna lie, it's not half bad. He must have picked up some tips from his mom.

Sweeping my paintbrush over my canvas, I grin. Tonight is already the best date I've ever been on and it's barely begun.

FOURTEEN
AXEL

IF I DIDN'T HAVE the pleasure of hearing Maisy's uninhibited, genuine laughter, I would have bolted at the first sign of Benoit in the poofy white shirt. He looked like a wannabe pirate or a man on an old-fashioned romance book my mother used to litter the end tables with.

I had no clue what the hell Francois was talking about with longing and nostalgia. For a long, agonizing moment, all I felt was panic and acute embarrassment.

But Maisy Stratford laughed, and everything changed. She allowed herself to get swept up in the moment, in the enthusiasm of Pam, in the spectacle of Benoit's sword brandishing.

And I reveled in *her*.

There aren't many women who could get me to stay in this class and paint a male model in a ridiculous shirt with an even sillier sword, but, it turns out, Maisy is one of them. I settle in for the long haul, soothed by her laughter, aware of every glance and grin she tosses my way.

Focusing on Francois's guidance, I give this whole portrait painting a real try. I outline Benoit's frame, adding more detail to his facial expression and the confidence he holds in his shoulders. However, while Pam spends most of the class focused on Benoit's pants, I skip that part of his body altogether.

I don't chance a glance, except to confirm that dude must be in pain. Britches ain't no joke and his are...painfully tight.

"Wonderful, Mr. Daire." Francois nods over my shoulder as he takes in my portrait. "You have a natural eye."

"Doesn't he?" Maisy pipes up beside me.

I turn to give her a look, my expression softening as I take in her smile. It's breathtaking and playful and makes my body relax. Being with her relaxes me in ways I haven't felt in years.

"Well, he is here with you, so yes," Francois agrees. A smooth talker, this one.

Maisy giggles and I fight the urge to roll my eyes.

We finish the class and relief mixed with a strange sense of regret washes through me. I don't want tonight to end. Maisy and I drank our wine and picked at the charcuterie board, and I want more. Conversation and long side looks and playful smirks.

"Want to hit the diner?" I ask, cleaning my last brush.

"I'd love to."

"Make sure you come back next week," Pam whispers, sidling up next to Maisy's canvas. "It's a nude lesson!" She claps her hands together.

Maisy's cheeks burn and her eyes dance. "Sounds riveting."

"It is," Pam agrees. "Hope to see you."

"Good to meet you, Pam," Maisy offers, noncommittally.

"You too, darling." She waves before exiting, making better time on her cane than she ought to.

"She's a hoot," Maisy comments.

"She's the type of grandmother grandkids wish for."

"Ah, my aspiration in life," Maisy laughs.

I tip my head. "You aspire to be a grandmother?"

"You know how some people peak in high school? Their glory years are their teens?"

I nod, knowing exactly what she means. I think of some of the guys I played hockey with back in high school. They're all good guys, some have families, some don't. But when I pass through my hometown, they're all telling the same stories, relieving the same moments from twenty years ago. "Yeah, I know some of them."

"Well, I'm certain I'm going to peak in my third act. Maybe my eighties."

I snort. "What?"

"I'm serious." Maisy grins but the look in her eyes is... well, serious.

"Okay." I frown.

"I want to do the family thing. Have a whole house filled with kids. I want to raise them and be at their football games—"

"Hockey games," I correct her.

She rolls her eyes. "And make dinner and quiz them for spelling tests. But when I'm a grandma...I want to paint and bake cupcakes and not worry about bedtimes and routine. I'm gonna peak in my third act, like Pam."

I bite back my smile. "Got it all planned out."

She shrugs. "Well, that used to be my plan. If it doesn't happen, I'm going to travel the world." She watches me curiously, biting her bottom lip. "Do you want to have more children?" Her tone is light, but her gaze is serious. She's not only asking out of curiosity.

The question pulls me up short. "I, I haven't really thought about it," I say slowly. Honestly. I mean, I guess with the right woman, with the right commitment, I could but...when have I had that until...maybe now?

Maisy grins, too big and too bright. She's backpedaling now. "Yeah, well, at least you have a shot at being a grandpa. You can peak in your third act too."

I nod, letting out a gruff laugh.

We thank Francois and Benoit and make our way out of the Art Attic. As I drive to the diner, Maisy's question loops in my mind.

Would I ever have more kids? Another family? Can I see myself getting married and having a more traditional life? The one I missed out on the first go-around?

I glance at Maisy, sitting in the passenger seat, her hands folded neatly in her lap, her expression thoughtful as she stares straight ahead.

Maybe. With a woman like her, with Maisy...maybe.

The realization doesn't scare me the way I thought it would, but it gives me pause. Because in a handful of weeks, Maisy Stratford has opened my mind to new ideas, to new ways of thinking, to the possibility of a different, better future than the lonely one I always envisioned. She's underlined the point Lola's been making for years: I need to "seek happiness." I can't live my life following in Lola's path.

I sigh, running my palm over the steering wheel. Maisy has opened my mind and maybe, even cracked the lock on my heart.

———

"WAIT, this was where you hung out in high school, wasn't it?" I tease Maisy as we slide into a booth in the back of the diner.

She laughs but her eyes confirm my theory. "There're three stoplights in the whole town," she says by way of explanation. "Thank God Knoxville is only forty minutes away."

"Hey, I grew up in a town just like this one. There's something to be said, to be admired, in places where neighbors look out for each other and kids grow up with tight bonds, together."

Maisy's expression softens. "Where did you grow up?"

"I'm from a small fishing village in Maine."

"Maine!" Her hand claps over her mouth, whether in surprise from my answer or from her reaction, I'm not sure. Either way, her blue eyes are filled with mirth, her cheeks pink with embarrassment.

"Not too far from Portland."

"Wow." She shakes her head, a few blonde strands falling from her bun.

"Why are you so surprised?"

She tilts her head, studying me. "I don't know. Now that I know the truth—"

"It's hardly a secret."

She giggles. The sounds tugs on something in my chest and I rub at it absentmindedly. Maisy Stratford is adorable. "Well, now that I know, I can see it."

I quirk an eyebrow.

"The sexy lumberjack vibe you could rock. I mean, if you traded your mock turtleneck for a flannel shirt. It's very Jason Momoa of you."

I open my mouth, prepared to groan, but instead, a

laugh falls out. An actual, real, genuine laugh that causes the corners of my eyes to crinkle.

Again, Maisy claps a hand over her mouth. Surprised. "You're laughing!"

Her reaction makes me laugh harder as I nod in agreement. "I do that sometimes."

"Twice tonight," she shoots back, her own laughter chiming in, mixing and blending, with mine.

It sounds nice, the two of us laughing in unison. More than that, it soothes me to know that we find the same things funny. That the easygoing conversation, the quips and jokes, I usually only have with Lola and Jasmine, or Asher, can be shared with Maisy too.

It feels like a win.

"So, you're from Maine, and then you moved straight to Seattle?" she asks tentatively.

"You googled me, didn't you?" I deadpan.

Her cheeks blaze and I relish the fact that I can make her blush.

Putting her out of her misery, I lean back in my seat. "Seattle came later. First, college in Minnesota. But I spent the majority of my career with the Rams in Seattle and now, here."

"Because of Lola."

"Yep. I'll probably just move anywhere she settles. When I was a kid, I thought Asher and I would live near each other, but he's never put down permanent roots so..." I shrug.

Maisy watches me for a moment, her gaze searching. Swept up with a touch of sadness.

"Hey, y'all, what can I get for you?" Our server appears, causing Maisy to snap out of her thoughts.

We order milkshakes and coffees, burgers and French fries.

Afterwards, I steer our conversation in a new direction. "Tell me something, Maisy."

"What?"

"Anything. Something...something no one knows." I'm going out on a limb here, but I like how spontaneous and in the moment she is. It's so different than anything I've ever known that tonight, at least, I want to try to be like Maisy. Live in the moment, ask the questions that spark my curiosity, just *be* with her.

"Well, I've told Mila this, but no one else really knows." She wrinkles her nose. "Okay, Mila and Cohen, because the three of us were having lunch."

"Okay," I say slowly, hating that the mention of Cohen's name causes my jaw to clench. They're friends; I know they're friends. But...how the hell can a man just be friends with a woman like Maisy?

She's incredible and at some point, if not already, Cohen's going to notice that. Hell, even River who probably couldn't find himself out of a paper bag gives Maisy sincere smiles and warm greetings when he sees her. If River Patton's figured it out, every straight man in Tennessee ought to be next. By logic alone.

"I want to move to Costa Rica," she announces, pulling me from my spiraling thoughts.

"What?" I sputter out, sounding a little too much like a dad. "The surfing camp?"

"Yes. I don't just want to visit. I want to move there. Well, first, oh, thank you." She smiles warmly at our server who drops off our burgers.

"You want to live there?" I prod after a long moment of

watching Maisy salt her fries and add a dollop of ketchup to her plate.

"Yes," she confirms, her eyes sparkling as they catch mine. "I think so; I've never been."

Huh? I frown. "How can you want to move someplace you've never been?"

She shrugs. "When you know, you know."

Internally, I groan. That's an answer Lola would flip my way. One I'd never accept but now...well, I can't tell Maisy that, can I?

"But my dad said something similar—"

Cue internal groaning again. Now, I sound like *her* dad?

"So, I want to go to the surf camp there first. At Witch's Rock."

"Witch's what?" I ask, my burger forgotten.

"Rock," Maisy says, her hands moving along with her words. She launches into a detailed description of the surf camp in Costa Rica, peppering it with day trips that include zip lining and yoga on the beach. It's the second time she's brought it up and I can tell it's important to her. That this trip, this potential move, is something she's thought a lot about. She concludes with, "Who wouldn't want to live there?"

I open my mouth to respond but...I've got nothing. Because the picture she painted, coupled with her in it, sounds pretty damn mesmerizing.

I clear my throat. "I've never been either."

Her eyes sparkle at my words. "Yet."

"Yet," I agree, feeling lighter after I admit it. Just because I haven't had a very spontaneous, live-in-the-moment life, doesn't mean I never will. As unsettled as Maisy's outlook leaves me, it's also exciting. She's thrilling and I like the way I feel when I'm with her.

My appetite returns and I pick up my burger, taking a big bite.

Maisy dunks a fry in her milkshake before popping it into her mouth. She shoots me a smile and I wink back, wanting to stay on this date forever. Wanting to learn as much as I can about Maisy Stratford and her big dreams.

When I drop her off at home, a sense of déjà vu rolls through me. I remember walking her up to her porch and kissing her lips after our not-so-great first date.

My palms grow clammy at the reminder, and I take the porch steps slowly, stalling.

Maisy spins toward me, her expression open, her face glowing. "Tonight was the best, Axe. Thank you."

"No, thank you." I stuff my hands in my pockets and rock back on my heels. "I had fun, Maisy. I had...more fun than I've had in a long time."

"Me too," she admits, shuffling a half step closer.

The scent of her perfume rolls over me and, screw it, I pull my hands from my pockets. Didn't I say I was going to live in this moment with her? Just *be*? I don't know what the future holds and I sure as hell don't want to rush it but... God, do I want to kiss this beautiful woman good night. Take a second to hold her close and slide my hands down her delectable curves.

"Maisy." My tongue swipes over my bottom lip. I clear my throat.

She tilts her head, studying me. "Do you want to come in?"

I feel the apology color my face as I swear softly. "I have an early skate tomorrow."

"Oh, okay." She looks down, steps back, and my chest twists painfully.

"Hey." My hand darts out, tucking under her chin and

lifting her face. Regret lines my words as I admit, "There's nothing I want more right now. Trust me."

A flicker of relief flares in her gaze. "I—"

Before she can voice anything else, I kiss her. I plant my lips over hers and get my first real taste of Maisy Stratford.

Intoxicating.

My hands glide up to hold her cheeks as she pitches forward, her hands wrapping around my wrists, holding on tightly. She whimpers as I deepen the kiss and I slip my tongue inside her mouth, my eyes closing as my tongue meets hers.

Maisy steps closer, her chest pressing into my abdomen as I lean down, arching over her. One arm wraps around her back, holding her steady, anchoring her. But my other hand slips into her silky tresses and holds the back of her head.

I kiss her fiercely and she melts into me, as sweet as honey. A whimper leaves her throat, and the sound rolls through me, kicking up my adrenaline and causing my need for her to spike. With one last tug of her hair, I force myself to step back.

My body is nearly buzzing with want for her. It's been so damn long since I've been with a woman who turns me on so quickly, intense like this.

"Maisy," I nearly growl, not wanting to leave her on her doorstep.

"I know," she murmurs. "Your skate." Her tone is gentle, her eyes still clouded over in the same lust and desire that color mine.

"My skate," I confirm, my voice wobbly.

Maisy steps forward and reaches up on her toes. I dip my head and we kiss, one sweet, simple, perfect kiss.

"Good night, Mais," I mumble against her mouth.

She pulls back and gives me that sweet smile. "'Night, Axe."

I wait for her to go inside, lock her front door, and turn on the lights. Then, I go home and take a long, cold shower that does nothing to relieve the ache snaking through my body.

That night, I dream of Maisy Stratford and the way she'd look in my bed, splayed out beneath me. It's the first dream I've ever wanted to become a reality.

It's the first dream I've ever had that's made me hopeful.

FIFTEEN
MAISY

"WAIT! HE WAS A PIRATE?" Mila snorts.

"More like an eighteenth-century wannabe aristocrat," I muse.

"Oh my God!" Mila laughs, the corners of her eyes twinkling.

Grinning, I lean forward. "I thought Axe was going to die."

She nods enthusiastically. "He's literally the last man I could envision in a paint and sip. Well, maybe River."

I laugh with her. "Axe was blushing like mad."

"Axe?" She lifts an eyebrow.

I shrug and then deflect. "And River would have been fine."

Mila rolls her eyes. "I don't know why you have such a soft spot for River Patton. The guy flipped a blueberry muffin tray onto your *breasts*."

I snicker. "It was an accident. And, I don't know, I... understand him. He doesn't fit in easily. I get that."

"Whatever." Mila shakes her head. "We're getting off topic. Was the date better than last time?"

"It was the best," I gush. Leaning forward over our table in the back corner of the Coffee Grid, I fill Mila in on the details. I tell her about Pam and Francois, the diner and milkshakes, and the smoking hot good night kiss on my front porch.

"But he didn't come in." She rolls her lips together, her expression thoughtful.

"He had a morning skate."

"Damn. He's traditional."

"Huh?" I frown. "I don't think he was making up the skate."

"No." She shakes her head. "He wasn't. I just think, it feels like he's *courting* you."

"All right, enough with the references to the eighteenth century."

Mila snorts again. "That's not what I meant. I think Axel is really taking his time with things, with you, because he likes you. He's...wooing you."

I lift an eyebrow but as I consider her words, they ring true. "Do you think it's...for real for real," I murmur quietly, my stomach knotting.

"When have you ever waited this long to have sex with a guy?"

I stick my tongue out at Mila. We both know the answer is never but, "You don't have to make me sound like a hussy."

"Now who's dating who?"

I laugh.

"And you know what I mean, Mais. When have you dated a man who puts this much thought into spending time with you and hasn't pushed for sex yet?"

"Never."

"Exactly. This thing with Axel is different. It's for real for real."

I smile. Mila's confirmation eases the band of worry that sits around my stomach, squeezing. For so long, I've wanted to belong. I've wanted to feel like I'm in it, for the long haul, with a true partner. Not someone I have to chase after, begging for crumbs of their attention. Not someone who tries to mold me into the vision they want me to be. But an *equal*. With Axel, it feels like I have a chance at finding that elusive happily-ever-after my heart craves.

"We should double date." Mila claps her hands together.

I squeal, nodding at my best friend. "Oh my God, yes! We haven't done that in ages!"

"Because Josh was a douchebag," she reminds me.

"And Avery was stuck up," I tack on.

"We wasted too much of our time on the wrong men," Mila laments.

"Totally," I agree, lifting my coffee mug. "To making better decisions."

She grins, clinking her mug against mine. "In life and in love."

"Amen to that." I take a sip of my coffee.

"I'll check with Devon about the team's schedule. We'll pick a night. Maybe Strickland's?" she asks, naming the top steakhouse in Knoxville.

"Ooh, yes," I agree. "We can even make a night of it."

Mila's eyes glitter and I groan, remembering her very detailed story of how Devon screwed her seven ways to Sunday against a hotel room window overlooking the city.

"Or not," I gag.

Mila shimmies. "We'll get rooms at Premier," she decides, naming her now favorite hotel.

"I'm happy for us. And not just because we're dating great men."

Mila's expression softens. "I'm happy for us too. Now, we can do couple things together. We're finally both in a good place, at the same time."

"Exactly." I grin, knowing she would understand.

"This is going to be the best!"

I bite my bottom lip, recalling Axel's good night kiss. "It already is."

———

AXEL AND DEVON WORK QUICKLY. Our double date at Strickland's is set up for the following Sunday, reservations confirmed at 6 PM. Because the team has a game on Saturday night, we opted for a Sunday night, knowing it would be quieter and less stressful. Plus, Devon and Axe can make it back to The Honeycomb for Monday's practice.

"What are you wearing?" Mila asks when I pick up the phone.

"Black leather skirt—"

"The one with the front slit?"

"That's the one."

"Damn," she mutters. "I have nothing cool to wear."

"Wear that denim dress with the red belt and nude sandals," I say, mentally flipping through her closet.

"Should I wear my hair straight or curly?" I ask, fingering my shoulder-length waves.

"Straight. I don't think Axel's ever seen your hair straight."

"He hasn't." I glance at my watch. "Okay, I need to move if I'm going to blow out my hair. See you at Strickland's?"

"Can't wait!" Mila squeals before hanging up.

I toss my phone down and hurry into my bathroom. Excitement courses through me. Knowing we're going to be with Mila and Devon, out with mutual friends, fills my cup with giddiness.

I adore Mila; I love being with her. For years, she was caught up in Avery. While Cohen and I were always friends and Mila would invite me to team outings, I never jived the same way I do with the Bolts. Avery never wanted to meet any of the guys I was dating out of the obligatory greetings. In the six years that Mila dated Avery, we double dated twice and both evenings were lackluster at best.

But tonight, the same energy and excitement that laces my girls' nights with Mila hangs in the air. I shower quickly, taking time to blow out my wavy hair and do a smoky eye. Then, I dress in my black leather skirt, sleeveless blush blouse, and strappy silver sandals. I opt for sparkly earrings and a big, statement necklace.

I'm swiping on lip gloss when a knock sounds on the door.

I wink at myself in the mirror, smiling at my own cheesiness. "You are a strong and confident woman," I remind myself.

The words hold more truth than they did a few months ago and the realization fuels my confidence.

Striding to the door, I pull it open, and my jaw nearly hits the ground.

Axel Daire could rival an eighteenth-century aristocrat as easily as a modern-day sex symbol. Like Jason Momoa.

He's dressed in black pants, his sculpted thighs on display. A black V-neck hangs off his frame, the neckline slouchy, showing off the strength of his chest. The material clings to his biceps and I bet if he flexed, he could knock

Josh out. His hair is pulled away from his face, tied into a neat man bun at the back of his head. His beard is trimmed, coating his chin and cheeks, and his full mouth parts on a hiss, eyes flashing. The sensations he emits roll through me like thunder.

Loud and forceful, demanding the attention of every nerve ending I possess.

"You're too fucking gorgeous for words." His voice is gruff, strained.

Sexy. That's how he makes me feel. Sexy and desired and...*wanted*.

Tilting my head, I rest it against the door. "Do you want to come in?" I'm playing it coy, something I've rarely done. But right now, I want to. I want to make Axel blush. I want to make him snap his restraint and forget all about his good intentions and wooing. I want him to scoop me up and kiss me hard and make me beg for all the things flickering in his midnight eyes.

Jesus. Where are these thoughts coming from? Just one look from Axel has my body reacting in ways that Josh sliding into me couldn't.

He blushes. The pink tint that spreads over his cheeks is endearing, especially since it's at odds with the rest of him. "Maisy, if I come in, we won't eat dinner tonight. At all." His words are low but filled with promise. His eyes are hard, shadowed with intent.

I shiver from his intensity and nod, my mouth too dry to form words. I reach for my purse as Axel bends down to retrieve my overnight bag. When he stands, his expression is softer, less rigid. He tosses me a wink. "You're more trouble than I pegged you as, Mais."

I grin. "I've never been called a troublemaker before."

"First time for everything." He extends his hand and I take it, letting him guide me to his truck.

When we're on the road, heading for Knoxville, I relax. I breathe in the masculine scent of his cologne, run my hand over the soft leather of his truck seats, and soak up the country music playing.

"When did you start listening to country?" I ask, rolling my head toward him. "It doesn't strike me as being popular in a small fishing village in Maine."

The corner of his mouth curls. "When Lol was born. Only thing that would put her to sleep."

"It stuck with you?"

"Yeah." He looks at me for a beat before turning back to the road. "It's all about fishing, drinking, and broken hearts."

I bite my bottom lip. "You ever have your heart broken, Axe?"

His neck snaps toward me, his eyes searching. After a moment, he rolls his lips together and nods. "By life, Maisy Stratford. Then by a woman."

"The two-year relationship?"

"Yeah," he admits. "Afterwards, I kept saying I couldn't date because the breakup was hard on Lola. It was. But it was also hard on me. Anna married Ben, grew her family. For a long time, I thought I could have that with Marisol—that's her name." He pauses, his eyes searching mine before turning back to the road. I sit riveted, my eyes zeroed in on his expression, not wanting to miss anything he's finally—finally!—sharing with me. "Marisol grew frustrated with my inability to commit. She said I wasn't giving her enough, wasn't as invested as her. We broke up and a year later, she was married with a baby on the way."

Ouch. His pain, his discomfort at sharing a vulnerability, rocks through me. "That must have been hard, Axel.

Especially if deep down, you were hoping for the same type of future." I phrase it as a statement, but really, I'm fishing. Does he want to marry and have a family one day?

Axel's quiet for a long moment and I worry I pushed too far. My fingers curl into my palms, my nails biting into my skin as I force the apology on the tip of my tongue to stay put and wait for his response.

"It was. It affected me more than I realized. But also not nearly enough."

Huh? "What do you mean?" I whisper.

His head swivels toward mine, slowly. Deliberately. "Marisol, our breakup, it hurt. But not the way losing you would. If there is a woman who could level me, Maisy, it's you."

I suck in a breath at his words. They're half plea, half truth. A vulnerability he's never given me before. For all my worries, I realize I also have the power to hurt Axel the same way he could hurt me.

"This is for real for real," I mutter.

He nods, flashing me his dark eyes. "Doesn't get more real than this, beautiful."

"I'm glad."

"Yeah?" He slides a palm over the top of the steering wheel. "So am I. That's why I want to take it slow."

Understanding dawns. The motives behind his wooing. Mila was right, we're *courting*. "Slow," I repeat. But now that I understand Axel's intentions, slow sounds good.

SIXTEEN
AXEL

I CAN BARELY FOCUS on the conversation at dinner. While it's comfortable and fun, with Maisy and Mila shooting each other wide smiles and having entire conversations through their facial expressions, I can't tear my eyes away from the gorgeous goddess beside me.

Maisy looks incredible in her flirty sundresses and sweet cardigans. But she's a vixen in leather, and my plan to take this slow, to be measured and practical, folds the more I drink in her sleek, straight, honey strands. And big blue eyes framed by the sootiest lashes I've ever seen. The straps of her sandals encircling her ankles and the hot pink polish on her toenails hypnotizes me. Everything about Maisy screams tonight.

And fuck, I want tonight.

But I also want tomorrow night and the night after that and... I can't think that far into the future. I just know that whatever story Devon is sharing doesn't hold a candle next to the sound of Maisy's laughter, or the flash of excitement in her eyes, or the way she tosses her hair over her shoulder.

God, she's mesmerizing. Breathtaking. *Mine*.

No, not mine yet. But I want her to be.

Devon kicks my shin under the table and I grunt. "Huh?"

"Is Lola coming to the Hawks game?" Mila asks. By the way her eyes dart to Devon's, I know this is the second, hell, maybe third, time she asked.

I shift in my seat, glancing at Maisy who looks at me curiously.

"She is." I direct my response to Maisy. "If you come, you can sit in the family box with her." The second the words are out of my mouth, a blaze of panic burns through me. Am I ready for this? Is Maisy? Mixing Maisy and Lola. Concocting opportunities for them to spend time together. I search her eyes; I don't want to push her.

"That's a great idea!" Mila's enthusiasm diffuses some of the nerves bundling at the base of my throat. "I'll be there."

"I'd love to." Maisy's voice is quiet, laced with her usual sweetness.

"It's next Thursday," Devon tosses out helpfully. He lifts his beer to his lips and takes a swig. "They're going to slaughter us, but at least you both will be there to cheer us up afterwards."

Mila rolls her eyes. "You might win."

Devon and I exchange a glance and I shake my head. "Maybe next season. But the Hawks are a well-oiled machine. We're going to go out there, play good hockey, and give it our all, but Austin Merrick has been leading the Hawks for years. They're not working out kinks the way we are."

"But the Bolts do have phenomenal leadership," Mila volleys back, her eyes locked on Devon. Our team captain.

"We do," I agree, tipping my head toward Devon. "And we'll get there."

"We will." He flashes me an appreciative smile.

As Mila pulls the conversation away from hockey, referencing some mutual friends of hers and Maisy's, I turn my focus back to my woman. My woman.

Tonight, I couldn't wait to get here, bring her to a hotel room, and see what unfolds between us.

Now, I can't wait to get out of here. I want to drive her home to my house and lay her down in the center of my bed and savor the hell out of anything she gives me. In my house. With her perfume infusing my sheets and strands of honey splayed on my pillowcase.

Shit. I shift again in my chair, uncomfortable as fuck. How the hell are we still on the appetizers? How long is this dinner going to last?

I glance at my beer bottle, still half full. If I'm going to take Maisy home tonight, I need to stop drinking. But will she want to go? Home with me? Tonight was about a double date, having fun with Mila and Devon. Right now, I couldn't care less about them. I just want the woman sitting beside me, shooting me sly grins with a pouty, full upper lip, to take me out of misery and let me try with her. All in, all the way.

"Here are your entrees," our server announces.

"Oh great!" Mila exclaims. "Wait till you see their dessert menu, Mais."

Maisy groans. "The turtle cheesecake."

"To die for," Mila agrees, thanking the server for her plate.

Across from me, Devon snickers. "Gonna be a long dinner, man," he mutters quietly.

The fucking longest.

———

WE SAY good night to Mila and Devon in the lobby of Premier, a swanky hotel I've never been to before. With hockey, I've stayed in some pretty nice places. But this, tonight, is different. Because I don't do this—drop money on five-star hotels for some type of staycation. I barely venture into Knoxville, preferring to stay close to the UT campus in case Lola needs me.

"You okay?" Maisy asks, her eyes shadowed with concern.

I let out a breath. "You're going to think I'm crazy." I take her hand and lead her away from reception, settling us onto two chairs in a seating area.

"What's wrong?" she whispers.

Our bags are still in the truck. I need to get them. I need to check in. But I want to take her home, to my home; fuck, I want this woman in my bed.

"You're having second thoughts," she murmurs.

"What?" I shake my head, trying to understand her words.

"You're not into this"—she gestures between us—"and you don't know how to tell me nicely that you don't want to stay here tonight." She stands up, wobbling slightly on her heels as a flash of anguish hits her eyes. "It's okay," she mutters. "We can go now and still be professional. No hard—"

"What are you talking about?" I nearly explode from my seat standing so quickly that I surprise Maisy. She stumbles back and I grip her upper arm to keep her upright. "You think I'm not into this? That I don't want you?" I shake her elbow a bit. "How the hell can you think that?"

Her mouth drops open, her eyes widening. "I, you, what?"

"Shit." I tug her back down, both of us sitting in our chairs. "Maisy, I want you so badly, I can't think straight."

"Then why would you not want to stay—"

"I want you in my bed," I practically growl. "I wanna wrap you up in my sheets. Spend the whole fucking night lost inside you and kiss you tomorrow in my kitchen over coffee. Not at some random hotel. Not for our first time together." I pause, trying to collect my thoughts. I never share this much, but I need her to understand. A wild, uncontrolled feeling rushes through me. I need her to understand that this isn't just casual.

I'm not fucking casual. I don't know what the hell I am, but with her, it's more than anything I've ever been in the past.

When I look up, blowing out a ragged sigh, Maisy's pupils are dilated. She's staring at me like she's never seen me before.

I'm messing this up. Coming on too strong. She just got out of a complicated relationship and isn't ready for this. For me going all caveman on her, laying shit out. I shouldn't do that anyway. Not when I could be a damn rebound to her and I'm sitting here wanting to be *not casual*.

"Fuck," I swear again, screwing my eyes closed. "Maisy, I—"

"Take me home, Axe," she cuts me off, her voice quiet but strong. Sure.

I open my eyes, wanting to confirm I'm reading this right. Does she mean my home or her home?

"Your home," she states, reading the question in my eyes.

A relieved puff of air leaves my lips and I pull her

toward me, pressing my mouth against hers. The kiss is hard, with an edge of need and a hint of desperation.

When I pull back, I stare into her eyes. "Are you sure, Maisy? Because if we do this, I can't keep things casual."

"I don't want casual."

"What do you want, sweetheart?"

She licks her lips, her chest rising and falling faster than it was a minute ago. "Everything. I want it all, Axe."

Her words light my blood on fire and my eardrums roar. My fingers feel like live wires, my entire body tuned and alert. My heart rate doubles. Concern flairs to life in my mind, a warning, a voice of reason.

Don't get in over your head. Take it slow. There's no need to rush.

I war with my thoughts, my head reaching for logic, my body pleading for now, this moment with this woman.

In the end, Maisy makes the decision easy. "How fast can you drive?"

I stand again, pulling her with me. "Let's get out of here."

Body wins, blocking out my mind. I escort my gorgeous date to my truck and drive home, my fingers laced through hers for the entire ride.

SEVENTEEN
MAISY

SHYNESS SWEEPS through me at the hunger in Axel's eyes. They're bottomless, black pools of desire edged in a want so strong, my blood heats.

For a man who conceals his thoughts and swallows his words, the naked appreciation he feels for me bowls me over. It's intense and sexy and desperate enough to make me *need* him.

His keys clink against the countertop as he purposefully places them down. He doesn't rush, doesn't move quicker. No, he continues to watch me, study me, his eyes as probing as they are caressing.

I work a swallow and shuffle back half a step. God, I want his onslaught. My toes curls in my strappy silver heels. I want it and yet...am I ready for a man like Axel?

Hell fucking yes, my head screams. But my heart does a stutter step because he's a life changer. Deep down, I know it as surely as I know my own name.

Axel Daire could ruin me. He's the man who can dash away my insecurities. Who can banish the thoughts that plague my mind. He's the man who can give me the whole

I'm searching for, but if he backs away, if it doesn't work out between us, the hole he'll leave will be a damn crater.

He tilts his neck to the side. His hand, large and calloused, rests palm down on the countertop. "We don't have to do anything."

I lick my bottom lip. "I want to."

The corner of his mouth tugs up in that half-smile I love even though I don't fully understand it. Don't fully understand him. "You sure? Tell me what you're thinking, Mais."

"You're too big for me," I blurt out the words, wincing as soon as they hit the air.

Axel snickers. A sound I hear so rarely, it makes me smile.

"I didn't mean big—" I backpedal, staring right at his package, which is more impressive then Benoit's. I lick my lips again.

"No?" he taunts, his eyes flashing.

"I mean, you are—"

Another snicker. His hand slips off the countertop. He steps toward me, deliberate.

I hold my ground, forcing myself to meet his eyes.

"You could break me, Axel. Emotionally. You could destroy me."

His hand cups my cheek, angling my face upward. "What if you destroy me first, Mais?" His breath fans over my lips, teasing.

"Not possible."

"Trust me, beautiful. It's not only possible, but likely."

I tip my head back farther, catching his eyes. He never lets down his guard. He's never vulnerable and yet, right now, Axel is baring himself completely.

"We don't have to do anything," he repeats. Another intentional step.

I move backward, my back pressing into the wall. "I want to. Really," I add, my hand closing around the wrist that holds my face. "I want to. Just..."

He lifts his eyebrows, waiting.

"Don't break my heart, Axe."

"Never," he growls. Then, his mouth lands on mine. Axel kisses me like a starving man. Desperate for a connection, for a physical touch. His kiss is commanding and deep. It knocks me off-balance and all I can do to keep up with him is hold on and fall into it.

I part my lips and his tongue delves inside, meeting mine in strong, certain strokes. Like everything he does, even his kisses are intentional.

Axel presses his hard body against mine and I melt, a groan ripping from my throat.

His breathing hitches and before I realize what he's doing, he's lifted me up and pinned me in place against the wall, his strong erection lined up with my core, his big palm supporting my ass.

"Wait—" *Put me down*, I want to shriek. I'm not the tiny, petite woman men toss over their shoulders. Or pin against hallway walls. "I'm too heavy."

Axel pauses for a moment, searching my eyes. Whatever he reads causes a swear to color the air between us. "You've never been with a real man, sweetheart. Let me show you how it's done." His voice is raspier, grittier than I've ever heard it. He grinds his erection against me, and I moan, my eyes closing, my head falling back against the wall.

"That's it; I got you," he says softly. Then, his lips are on my neck, his hand is in my hair, and I lose all the inhibitions I had a moment ago.

Axel's mouth moves over my skin like he's committed to

making this moment my sexual awakening. I've been with men, from high school to now, but none of them made me feel like a goddess in mere minutes.

Axel's hand cups my breast and I arch into him, my nipple poking through the lace of my bra and thin material of my shirt. He presses into me, and my hips tilt up to meet him.

"You sure, Maisy?"

"Please," I whimper.

With a movement so smooth, I don't see it coming, he spins me away from the wall and carries me, like it's nothing, to his bedroom. He places me down gently and his eyes find mine in the moonlight streaming through his windows.

His expression is severe. Solemn. I know that as big as this moment is for me, he feels the same way. It's humbling, to know Axel trusts me as much as I trust him.

His hands hitch around the band of my skirt and I lift my hips as he rolls it down my body. His eyes snag on the creamy lace between my thighs and his lips part. He reaches forward slowly, shifting the material to the side and dragging two fingers through my folds.

I close my eyes, the slightest touch igniting my body. Nerves coil deep in my belly, my heart races, blood pumping in my ears.

Axel shifts my panties back in place and my eyes pop open in time to watch him suck my arousal off his fingers. "Sweet as you."

I gulp, my mouth dropping open.

"We'll get there," he promises, moving over my body like a panther, smooth and steady.

I reach for the button on his pants. He drags the straps of my blouse off my shoulders. My skin heats under his touch and his body rolls over mine. He undresses me slowly.

When I'm in my thong and strapless bra, I shift onto my knees, face him, and reach out.

I drag the hem of his shirt up his torso, my core clenching, wanting, as his abs appear. When his shirt clears his head, I trace his pecs, my fingertips featherlight as I explore his smooth skin, his coiled strength.

He sucks in a breath but holds still, letting me have this moment. It's sensual, intensifying my need while also bringing me unknown pleasure. Who knew this—gentle touching, sweet kisses—could feel so erotic?

I place a kiss to the side of Axel's neck and he snaps, springing toward me like a leopard and laying me out beneath him.

"My turn," he explains before dipping his head and pulling my breast into his mouth, lapping and licking until my thighs clench together. I'm needy for release and if I wasn't so comfortable with him, I'd be embarrassed by how quickly he worked me up.

As if sensing my need, Axel moves down my body. "Not yet," he mutters before his face disappears between my thighs.

"Axel." I buck off the bed, about to come from one taste alone.

"You're so fucking sexy, Maisy," he mutters before dragging his tongue over my clit again.

I moan, loudly. Honestly. "That's how you make me feel," I warble, admitting the truth.

His heavy hand slides up my body and tweaks my breast. "Always." He sucks gently. "You should always feel like a fucking goddess."

I shatter against his tongue as his words wrap around me. More than his words is the sincerity, the absolute certainty, with which he says them.

He yanks my underwear off the tops of my thighs and loses his boxers. His erection springs free and I groan because it's fucking massive. "You're huge."

He chuckles. "You said that already."

"Yeah but...holy shit." My thighs clench together, desperate for the sweet relief Axel can provide.

Axel's fingers sweep along my cheek. "I got you, Maisy."

My hand darts out and curls along his shaft, pumping his long length.

He swears but holds still. "Not gonna last long if you keep touching me like that."

I let out a shaky breath and lay back, positioning myself beneath him. He rolls on a condom and lines up at my entrance.

His eyes hold mine. For a moment, we drown in each other. Our eyes convey all the words, all the meaning, all the things we haven't yet said. Then, Axel pushes into me, and I moan, arching upward.

"Fuck, you're incredible," I cry out, stretching to accommodate him.

He snorts. "Got nothing on you, beautiful."

He stills. I smile.

Then, he begins to move, and I clutch at him, gripping his arms as he rocks into me, slow, steady, and sure. Axel brings us to the peak of pure ecstasy and when I cry out again, he follows close behind me. Both of us tumbling down into the gentle touches and sweet kisses of each other.

It's more sensual than any experience I've ever had. It's more meaningful than any time before him. It's the most honest sexual moment of my life.

"Thank you, Axel," I mutter into his neck as he holds me against his chest.

"Shh." His fingers stroke my back. "Me and you, we're

just beginning, Maisy. This is only the start."

I smile against his warm skin and fall asleep in his arms, wishing I could stay there forever.

———

"HOW'D YOU SLEEP?" Axel's morning voice is raspy. It hits me right between my thighs, still sore from our night together.

I roll over, smiling when his face comes into view. "I like your bed."

He smiles. Smiles! One of those rare moments when his face opens up like a sail catching wind. It's glorious. "I like you in my bed." He swipes his mouth over mine. "I'm gonna try to keep you here."

"I'm in," I say. Although my tone is light, my meaning isn't. As far as Axel's concerned, I'm all in. I want to wake up in his bed, hold his hand, and feel his giant body move over mine every damn day for the rest of my life.

Glorious.

"Breakfast?" he asks.

"Coffee."

"And that." Axel moves from the bed, taking a moment to flip the sheet over my naked breasts. "Don't want you cold."

I smile at his thoughtfulness and watch his broad shoulders and fine ass as he tugs on a pair of sweats and makes his way into the kitchen.

On the nightstand, my phone beeps with an incoming message. It's probably Mila wondering why the hell I ghosted her last night. I bite my inner cheek to keep from laughing. I know as soon as I tell her the real reason, she's going to be as excited as I am.

I stretch my arms overhead, enjoying the jelly feel of my limbs. Last night was one of the best nights of my life. It was the most intimate, raw connection I've shared with a man. Axel's eyes held mine captive, drawing out emotions I've kept locked up, coaxing out wanton moans I never thought I'd make in the presence of a man.

Sex with Axel made me realize just how paltry my sexual encounters have been. Unsatisfying. Until this weekend, I've had more fun with my vibrator than with a man. I used to wonder if there was something wrong with me but now, to my greatest relief, I realize it was the men I've been with.

Selfish lovers.

But Axel is the most generous man I've ever known.

My phone beeps again and I swipe it up, my eyes scanning the screen.

Missy: Mom and Dad are having Sunday dinner next week. Mom's going to call you later today but please come.

I frown, trying to read the subtext. My parents host a family Sunday dinner one or two times a month, and while I always do my best to show up, I can't make every dinner. But Missy rarely begs me to make an appearance.

A flicker of unease runs through me. Did something happen with Dad's job? Is Mom sick? Is—

Missy: Brennan's parents are coming too!

Ah, I laugh. Missy and Brennan have been together for two years and while our parents know each other, they haven't consolidated Sunday dinners.

Me: Meet the families already? This is getting serious.

Missy: (Three Engagement Ring Emojis)

My mouth drops open. I adore Brennan but Missy is so young, and they don't need to rush into anything.

Me: You think?

Missy: I hope.
Me: EEP!
Missy: Next Sunday?
Me: Be there. Promise.
Missy: LOVE YOU
Me: YOU MORE

I drop my phone next to me and rest my head on the pillow, staring up at Axel's ceiling fan. It whirs slowly, lazy and gentle, like a breeze in the Deep South on a hot summer day.

Missy might get engaged. Married. A strange tension radiates over my shoulder blades, pulling at the center of my spine, at the thought. My stomach knots and a horrible thought invades my mind.

Am I jealous? Of my baby sister?

No. I'm just...worried. She's only twenty-three and... *and I thought I'd be married by twenty-three.*

My parents were high school sweethearts. They made long-distance work throughout college, married their senior year, and had me the following spring. Missy came along five years later and by the time my mom was my age, she was married, a homeowner, with two sweet daughters in dresses and bows.

I'm twenty-eight and until last night, never had a decent orgasm that wasn't self-induced. It's not that I'm not happy for Missy, because I am. She's my sister and she deserves a beautiful life with the man of her dreams. Deep down, I know that man is Brennan.

It's just that she's following the path I always envisioned for myself and I'm...pathless. Still talking about a fun move to Costa Rica the way I have been since college, thwarting off questions about my lack of a serious relationship. My lack of a fulfilling career. My lack of a certain future.

Can I have that with Axel? The man is nothing if not purposeful. He's an overthinker, an overanalyzer and yet... he hasn't hinted at anything *permanent* between us. Just not casual.

It's too early, my mind screams at me. *You're supposed to be enjoying this. This is the fun part!*

Isn't this the part I wished and waited for? The sleepless nights wrapped up in strong arms? Days filled with fun plans out or lounging around, together. There's no tension with Axel the way there was with Josh. I don't need to walk on eggshells around him or guard my thoughts.

He swears as he drops a pan in the kitchen. If I didn't receive Missy's message, I'd be out there right now, helping him make breakfast. That's what I *should* be doing.

Blowing out a sigh, I swing my legs to the edge of the bed and stand. Taking in the rumpled sheets and tossed pillows, I remind myself that last night was glorious. And today will be too, if I don't ruin it with my sour thoughts.

Missy deserves every happiness the same way I do. Why shouldn't I try to find that with Axel?

I open one of his drawers and pull out a Bolts T-shirt. Slipping it over my head, I love that it hits me mid-thigh, hanging loose around my middle. Only a man like Axel could make me feel dainty and feminine.

Only Axel has made me feel sexy.

Right now, I need to focus on that. Cherish it.

"You need some help?" I ask as I clear his bedroom and step into the kitchen.

He turns and grins, his bare chest more appetizing than the delicious scent of freshly brewed coffee. "What do you think?"

"You look good in the kitchen."

He snorts and reaches for me, picking me up and setting

me on the countertop. Making me feel as weightless as a feather. Some of my doubts from a few minutes ago disappear in his presence.

"You look better in my kitchen," he muses, frying up some eggs. "But I sure like cooking for you, Maisy."

I smile and when he passes in front of me, my legs dart out, wrapping around his waist and pulling him closer.

He chuckles, coming to stand between my thighs. He plants his big hands down, one on each side of my hips, and stares straight into my eyes, all the way down to my soul and the insecure, nagging thoughts that live there.

Then, he kisses me. Soft and reverent. Sweet. He kisses me like he knows I need the reassurance. He gives it, him, so freely that the backs of my eyes burn.

"How do you always know what I need?" I whisper when he pulls away.

"I'm observant." He turns off the stove and plates our eggs.

"It's more than that." I hop off the counter, grabbing the forks and napkins.

He stops in his tracks and stares at me. "I care about you, Maisy."

His words are as soothing as they are thrilling. "You're the most honest man I know."

He shakes his head, a sadness entering his gaze. "You need to raise your bar."

I laugh but he doesn't smile. Instead, he balances our plates in one hand and takes mine in the other, bringing me to the table.

Then, we sit and eat breakfast like a real couple. And everything from this morning, from Missy's messages, fade away. Instead, I live in the now and it's fucking glorious.

EIGHTEEN

AXEL

"SINCE WHEN DO you eat Thai food?" Lola asks me, closing the refrigerator door.

"Hey, easy with that," I remind her, checking that the door is still on the hinges. She rolls her eyes and swipes a fork, eating the pad Thai leftovers cold. "Give me that." I swipe the takeout container and put it into a bowl, popping it into the microwave. "Swear, if I didn't look out for you, you'd never eat."

Lola laughs and pops the tab on a Diet Coke. When I hand her the bowl, properly heated, she breathes it in appreciatively. "This is good Thai too, not the quick takeout kind." She quirks an eyebrow.

"Maisy brought it over for dinner the other night."

"Wow. You're really branching out, huh?"

I refill my coffee cup and sit across from her. "What do you mean?"

"Thai food, going into the city..." She gestures at me. "Your appearance."

"What's wrong with my appearance?" I snap.

Lola laughs. "Nothing. That's my point. You look good, Dad. Happy."

I dip my head in acknowledgment. "I am. Happy," I confirm quietly. The time I've been spending with Maisy has infused a lightness in my life that hasn't existed in years. I look forward to seeing her, think about her constantly, and wish I could stop time when we're together. With my schedule and a handful of away games, it seems like we never have enough time.

"And she's broadening your horizons," Lola adds.

I grunt, not wanting to tell my kid that the new woman in my life has introduced me to more ideas and outlooks, cuisines and cultures, than I've experienced in the past decade. Not since Marisol. "I'm a creature of habit."

"Maisy is good for you." Lola points her fork at me.

I take a swig of coffee in response and Lola smiles.

"She's sitting with you in the family box on Thursday."

"Nice!" Lola exclaims, looking genuinely excited about spending one-on-one time with Maisy.

"You cool with that?"

"More than cool, Dad. I want to get to know her. I like her."

"Yeah."

Lola rolls her eyes at my inability to have a deep conversation about my romantic life. But that's not the type of thing a dad needs to discuss with his daughter. As long as she's okay with my dating and I get a pulse on her feelings toward Maisy, we don't need to hash out every detail and date the way Lola would with Jas.

Lola chuckles again, standing from her chair.

"Bowl in the dishwasher," I remind her.

She rolls her eyes but picks up her bowl and fork, rinses

them, and places them in the dishwasher. Turning to face me, she says, "Don't forget about family weekend."

Shit! I take a big gulp of coffee to cover up the fact that I did forget. With my hockey schedule, and now, trying to squeeze in time with Maisy, I haven't checked in with Lola as much as usual. Other than our Sunday brunches, our conversations have taken place through text messages. "I'm looking forward to it."

She laughs. "You forgot."

"I did not," I fib.

Lola shakes her head, her expression softening. "I'm happy for you, Dad."

"Thanks, Lol."

"Anyway"—she swipes up her purse—"I'm going to meet Jasmine. Mom, Ben, and the boys land next Friday night. Mom's making reservations at Clint's and then, Saturday is all the family stuff on campus."

"Sounds good." I stand. Walking over to Lola, I place my coffee mug in the sink and kiss my daughter's forehead. "I'm glad your mother is taking the lead on reservations."

Lola snickers, knowing Anna is the one who keeps up with all the details in her life. I make sure her car is running the way it should and that she's got proper health insurance, but Anna is the one who schedules dinner reservations and sends flowers on the first day of final exams. Together, we've made a pretty incredible co-parenting team. "I'll see you later, Dad."

"See you, Lol." I stand by the door and watch as Lola slips into her car and pulls out of the driveway. She honks once and I lift my hand in farewell.

Pulling out my phone, I open the calendar app and note family weekend. Knowing I won't be able to spend it with Maisy, a strange desperation to see her rolls through me.

Me: Hey, you got plans tonight?
Maisy: Grabbing dinner with my sister, then free.
Me: Want to watch a movie?
Maisy: Aren't we too old for code lingo?

I snort at her honesty. Hell yeah, we're too fucking old for it. But what do I text her? *I want you to come over so I can fuck you hard and hold you all night?*

Me: Spend the night with me?
Maisy: I'd love to. Your place or mine?
Me: I don't want to rush your night. Come over when you're done with dinner. I'll be here.
Maisy: See you tonight. (Kiss Emoji)

I blow out a sigh, relaxing now that I'll see her tonight. I've never felt this way about a woman before, twisted up and turned inside out. I thought I had this with Marisol, but in hindsight, our relationship paled in comparison. It was the breakup that gutted me. Watching Marisol move on, much the way Anna did, left me wondering if I'd ever find a partner. Left me feeling like I was the problem, the person lacking in the relationship.

With Maisy, I have a chance at real happiness, at a stable future, again. I won't take that for granted. Besides, I haven't felt her curves or tasted her mouth in two days, and that's two days too damn long.

Hell, even waiting until tonight feels too long.

Lifting my phone again, I call Beau Turner.

"What's up, Brawler?" He picks up on the first ring.

"Want to get a lift in before practice?"

"Sure, I gotta get out of my house anyway."

I frown. "What's going on?"

"My little sister gets into town this weekend. Gran is over the moon and on a cleaning spree."

"Ah," I say sympathetically. I've only met Turner's

Gran a handful of times, but at nearly ninety, the woman is a force to be reckoned with. She may look sweet and frail, but her mind is sharper than a tack and her language more colorful than a box of crayons. "Meet you at the gym?"

"Be there in thirty."

I hang up, letting out another sigh. I feel restless, too much pent-up energy and nowhere to put it. A workout, followed by a grueling practice, will do my mind good. Otherwise, I'll spend the entire afternoon thinking of Maisy and staring at the clock, counting down the hours until she's with me.

———

"YOU LOOK DIFFERENT," Damien Barnes remarks as I sit down on a bench in the locker room.

"Different?" I tug off my practice jersey, soaked through with sweat.

Barnes narrows his eyes, studying me. For a second, he reminds me of Mom. If she was still here, she'd have pegged my feelings for Maisy before I admitted them to myself. "Chipper," Barnes remarks.

I laugh. A big, shoulder-shaking, loud laugh.

The locker room quiets as the team stares at me. Cole Philips' mouth is hanging open. Turner looks amused, River skeptical. Their reactions make me laugh harder. Has it been that long since I've truly laughed? Have I never showed them that deep down, I'm a fun guy? Or at least, I possess the capability to *become* fun?

I swipe a hand over my beard, my laughter subsiding. Shaking my head, I pull a pair of shorts from my locker. "That was pretty fucking chipper," I remark.

Turner chuckles as Philips draws his mouth closed.

"Definitely different," Barnes mutters. "What's going on with you?"

"He's in love," Devon offers.

I glare at him. "I'm seeing someone," I correct.

"Maisy?" Turner guesses.

River glowers at me.

I stand up straighter, turning to face my team. "Yes. We're...dating."

"Very adult of you." Barnes smirks, but his eyes are serious. "You really like her." He says it like a statement, which it is. It's the truth.

"I care about her," I admit, glancing around at the guys. "She's a good woman. And you all—" I begin, pointing at them.

Devon grabs my finger and twists it. "We know how to treat Maisy. Everyone here has been nothing but respectful toward her. We don't need to hear any more of your lectures." He lifts his eyebrows, his eyes silently calling me out for how many times I've reminded the group not to look twice at Lola.

Sighing, I realize he's right and drop my hand. Not before I glare at Patton, but that's because the kid deserves it. I know he and Maisy have something easy between them, an acquaintanceship or some shit, but that doesn't mean I like him any more than the first time I met him. So, not much at all.

"Good for you, man." Turner claps me on the back.

"Yeah," Philips pipes up. "I like Maisy. She's so friendly and always smiling."

"She is," I agree, knowing my woman brings warmth and sunshine wherever she goes. Even to miserable miscreants like Patton.

"She's a damn miracle worker if she can get you to laugh like that," Barnes says.

A few guys on the team titter, but I laugh again. Loud and boisterous. "Ain't that the truth?" Since I've met Maisy, my life has been fuller. Fucking Barnes is right. I *am* chipper.

After leaving The Honeycomb, I head home. I take a long shower, cook some mushroom risotto and green salad, and collapse on my couch. I watch a documentary about sharks, killing time until my doorbell rings.

When I pull the door open, my beautiful woman stands on the porch. Her hair is in a low ponytail, bright yellow and blue earrings hanging from her ears and dusting the tops of her shoulders. She's wearing a ruffly blouse and a flirty skirt and I can't wait to peel it all off her.

"Hey," I mumble, closing the space between us. I plant my mouth on hers, pulling her over the threshold and closing the door behind us.

Maisy's hands move up my arms, her palms caressing my beard before holding my cheeks. She kisses me back. Sweet turns into needy.

I sweep her into my arms, and she laughs, leaning her head back. Her eyes find mine as I move us into my bedroom. "What did I do to deserve the royal treatment?"

I place her down in the center of my bed. "You always deserve the royal treatment." I pull my shirt clear off my head.

Maisy's pupils dilate as she stares at my bare chest, her eyes tracking my movement.

"How much you drink?" I ask, not seeing her car out front.

"Not a lot. Missy dropped me off."

I crawl over her. "How much?"

She rests her head on a pillow. Her arms snake around my neck and her knees fall open, her skirt riding up her thighs. "I feel completely sober right now."

I place an open-mouthed kiss on her cheek, dragging my lips over to meet hers. "Completely sober?"

"Yes," she moans as I brush my fingers up her exposed thigh. My hand finds the delicate zipper on her hip and I drag it down. "I missed you, Axe."

"I told the team about us."

Her eyes pop open, a flicker of something I can't read flaring to life. "What'd they say?"

"Happy for us," I calm her mind, dropping my mouth to her neck.

She arches into me, and I love it, the press of her breasts against my bare chest, the feel of her skin under my palm.

"Are you?" she murmurs.

I pull back, note the seriousness in her gaze. My eyebrows snap together.

"Happy?" she clarifies.

My mouth curls into a smile, something I'm doing a hell of a lot more of lately. "More than I ever remember being."

Maisy blows out an exhale, as if she was holding her breath. "Me too."

"Good." I kiss her hard.

Her skirt bundles around her stomach as she wraps her legs around my waist. I sink into the space between her thighs, loving on her so damn good.

We spend hours wrapped up in my sheets, showing each other just how damn happy we are. How happy we can make each other.

It's more than I've ever known exists.

NINETEEN
MAISY

"SO..." I stare at Axel over the rim of my coffee mug.

"So?" He leans back in his seat, waiting.

"You guys need anything else?" Jas asks at the end of our table.

"No, thanks." I smile at Jas, pointing to my nearly empty plate. "The waffle was amazing."

"Right? It's a new recipe," she informs me.

"Well, tell the chef it's delicious."

"Will do." She flashes us a grin as she stacks our plates.

When Jasmine is gone, Axel leans closer. "So?"

I pull in a deep breath and let it out. Axel and I are dating and the team knows about us but... "My parents are having a dinner on Sunday."

"Okay," he says slowly, his eyes searching mine.

"Would you like to go with me?" I fight the urge to squeeze my eyes closed. Things with Axel are new and going well. I don't want to rock the boat or put pressure on our relationship.

Does he want to meet my parents? I think of Dad and his easygoing smile and friendly jokes. But Mom, what will she think about Axel? What will she think—worse, say—about Axel and me as a couple?

Will she think he's too mature and experienced for me, the woman who can never hold a man? Will she comment on his having a daughter? On him being a hockey player, and by extension, a playboy?

The thought heightens my nerves. Will she embrace my dating him, or minimize the happiness I've found? My parents have always had an open-door policy, but they're not used to me bringing a man around. Part of the reason I don't is because of Mom's judgement.

Josh hated Sunday dinners and rarely accompanied me. In fact, I began skipping them too, just to avoid the questions and my mother's look of disapproval. Crap, that should have been another sign, huh?

Axel twirls a pepper shaker. "What time?"

"What?" I focus on him.

"What time is dinner?"

"Oh, we usually eat around 6 PM so I aim to get there around five. Missy's boyfriend, Brennan, and his parents are coming."

Axel shrugs. "Sure. I can be there."

His response is unexpected. A flutter of nerves leaves my body at his confirmation that he'll come, but he doesn't give anything else away. Is he excited? Nervous? Only coming to appease me? Is meeting the parents even a thing when you're thirty-six with an adult child?

"Do you have something else on Sunday?"

He grips the back of his neck, shrugging again. "I've got some stuff over the weekend. It's family weekend at UT."

"Oh, that's right! It's such a great time. They do a lot of fun activities up on campus. One year, they did a firepit with s'mores. That was a big hit."

Axel gives me his half-smile again. "But I can do Sunday. I'll pick you up."

"Okay." I smile, feeling better about his response now that I know he has a stacked weekend with Lola's school stuff. Plus, his game on Saturday afternoon.

The fact that after such a busy weekend, he'd come to my family home for dinner means a lot. "Thank you, Axel."

His eyebrows pull together. "Sure. It's no biggie."

"Right," I agree, his words causing my burst of happiness to fade. Is meeting my family not a big deal because it doesn't mean as much for him as it does to me? Or is it not a big deal because it's a given that he would meet them since our relationship is progressing?

Stumped, I pick up my coffee mug and take another sip. Axel is the first relationship I've been in where I feel like I'm on equal footing. He treats me amazing, shows me how much he wants and desires me, and I'm as comfortable with our conversation as I am with our silence.

I need to stop overanalyzing. I'm in a good place and our relationship is moving in a great direction.

Axel calls Jasmine over to ask for the check.

As he pays, I can't help but study him, trying to understand the subtext of his easy acceptance—or was it a brush-off—about meeting my parents. I can't help but squash the little voice in my head that raises a slew of old insecurities.

You are strong and confident, I push back, trying to quench the uncertainty that floods my limbs.

Everything is fine. Great, even.

But as I slip into Axel's truck and buckle up, I can't shake the feeling that something is amiss. That something is off between us. It sticks with me for the rest of the week, making me question my new relationship. Making me question myself.

———

"IT'S great to finally meet you!" Indiana Scotch, Coach Merrick's niece and Coach Scotch's wife, maneuvers her son Fox in her arms to shake my hand.

"You too." I smile at her before dropping my gaze to her sweet baby. "And you too, Fox."

Indy bounces the baby in her arms.

"Indy!" a voice hollers.

We look down into the stands and I spot a gorgeous blonde with bright blue eyes waving both arms over her head. She's hopping up and down to get Indy's attention.

Indy snorts. "That's my cousin, Claire. It's so weird, playing against the Hawks."

"Oh, that's right," I murmur, recalling that Noah played for the Hawks until his retirement. Now, as a coach for the Bolts, he's facing off against his former teammates, and family. His brother is a winger for the Hawks and Indy's cousin Austin is the Hawks captain. "This must feel surreal."

"Totally," Indy laughs. Fox begins to fuss in her arms.

"Indy!" Another woman waves.

Fox begins to cry.

"I can rock him for a bit, if you want to go visit with your cousin and friends," I offer, hoping I don't come across as desperate.

But Indy doesn't look panicked by my offer. Instead, relief floods her expression. "Really? You sure you don't mind? He'll calm down in a minute or two but—"

"It's fine." I reach for baby Fox. "I got him. We'll be right here." I glance around, since we're in the family box, surrounded by the wives, girlfriends, and family members of the Bolts.

"Thank you so much, Maisy. I'll be right back." She passes me the baby.

"Take your time." I cradle Fox in my arms, looking down at his red cheeks and wide eyes. "I got you, little man," I murmur. Relocating to a quieter corner of the box, I rock him in my arms, whispering soothing words.

He's a beautiful baby, with the same deep, chocolate brown eyes as his daddy. I can't tear my eyes away from the gentle curves of his cheeks, the adorable slope of his nose. As I sway with him in my arms, he lets out the cutest yawn, and his eyes begin to close. He fights his sleep, whimpering every few seconds, until he settles. When he's asleep, I cradle him closer, wanting to shut off the noise of the booth.

"You're a natural," a woman remarks.

I glance up into the perceptive eyes of an elderly woman I've never met.

I chuckle and shake my head. "I don't know about that."

"I do. How many kids do you have?"

"Oh, no, he's not mine. I, I'm not a mother."

"Yet," she says gently, slipping her glasses more firmly up her nose. She glances out toward the ice. "I had six. That's why I have so many wrinkles."

"Six kids?"

She laughs. "Yes. And seventeen grandchildren."

"Wow!" I gasp.

She shakes her head. "But no great-grandchildren close by. My granddaughter, Rose, has three kids but they live in California, so I don't see them often. And my grandson, Peter, has two but his wife is from Argentina, and they live there now. I wish Beau would settle down and give me some sweet babies, but I don't think that's in the cards."

I grin at her honesty. "Beau Turner?"

"Yep." She gestures toward the ice. "He's my son Gerald's eldest. Eldest of five."

"Really?" I tilt my head, looking out onto the ice. Beau is in goal and suddenly, I see him in a new light. The eldest of five; I can't imagine. I think the constant comparisons between Missy and me are difficult to manage. Imagine having three other siblings to contend with?

"Yes," she sighs heavily. "It was hard on him, losing his parents." The wrinkles in her cheeks deepen as the grief she's kept hidden travels over her expression. "It was hard on all of us, but Beau, he took it the worst. Did everything he could to keep his siblings looked after." She lets out a sound, a cross between a chuckle and a sob. "To look after me too." Her blue eyes find mine again, the wisdom in them looming. "That's why he enlisted."

"I, I didn't realize Beau served."

"Afghanistan," she offers. "Having him back has been a blessing for me. Not for him, I'm afraid." She rolls her lips together. "I'm not much of a partier these days, although back in my day, I could shake it with the best of them." She gives a little shimmy and a wink.

I smile.

"But," she continues, sobering, "he needs time, and space, for himself. My granddaughter, Beau's sister, is moving back this weekend and she's going to stay at the house with me. It will be good. For all of us." She tilts her head. "At least I fucking hope so."

I laugh, her profanity catching me off guard, but my heart is heavy with the loss she experienced. In my arms, Fox snores softly. His weight, his warmth, nestled against my chest feels more significant than it did a moment ago.

Will I become a mother one day? Will my relationship with Axel develop into a family? I've always seen myself having children... If I want a future with Axel, we would need to discuss it. His response when I asked was vague and nothing to bank on.

We need to discuss so many things.

I look back to the ice and Axel, the big, imposing, giant of a man stops his warm-up to catch my eye. We stare at each other for a long moment, his expression severe, eyes zeroed in on me cradling Fox.

Does he see a future with me? One with kids and a noisy house?

"Hey!" Lola appears at my side. Her fingers stroke Fox's head gently. "I'm glad you came."

"Hi!" I turn to smile at her and introduce her to Beau's gran.

When I look back to the ice, Axel's in position, his body alert, his focus solely on the game. What was that? Did my holding Fox scare him? Snap something into focus, the same way it did for me?

"You're a lifesaver, Maisy." Indy grins. "Thanks for getting him to sleep. I can take him if you want."

I look down at Fox for a heartbeat. "I can hold him a little longer."

To be honest, I could hold him the entire game. I've always known I wanted to create a family but tonight, that reality slid more into focus. I've always pictured myself getting married and having children but now, an eagerness to start the life I've wished for fills my veins.

"He's adorable," Lola whispers.

I ease into the seat beside her. "He really is," I agree. "How are classes going?"

"Good," Lola says. "This weekend is family weekend."

"Oh, that's right. Are you excited?"

"Totally." She takes a sip of her soda, raising her hand toward me. "Are you coming to dinner tomorrow?"

"Dinner?" I tip my head to the side.

"Yeah. My mom, stepdad, and brothers are flying in. We've got reservations at Clint's." She rolls her eyes. "Mom wanted to stay close to campus so we don't miss any of the events Saturday morning. Dad told you, right? I checked that he was free weeks ago. He usually volunteers at the Children's Hospital the second Saturday of the month, but I think he switched with someone."

Her words land in my stomach like boulders, weighing me down and crushing the hope I was beginning to feel about my future with Axel. He volunteers at the Children's Hospital? Why wouldn't he tell me that? Why wouldn't he invite me to tag along?

More than that, why wouldn't he invite me to his family dinner on Friday night when I just invited him to Sunday dinner? I handed him the perfect opening and he...said nothing.

Fox fusses in my arms and I reposition him, feeling like my dream of motherhood is fading away again.

"He must have forgot." I shrug, feigning casual.

"Ugh," Lola groans. "So like him. Anyway, classes are good, but I've got this one professor..."

I nod as she launches into a story about her professor. I can't focus fully on the story because inside, my disappointment is swelling. The unease I've felt all week magnifies, eating up space in my mind until it's the only thing I can think about.

Do I want a more serious relationship than Axel does? Does my vision of our future not align with his?

Hasn't he given me the signs, showed me, that he wants more too? That this is for real for real? He told me it is!

Fuck. What if he never wants to get married or have more children?

Is it too early to have these conversations? Is it irresponsible, setting us both up for heartache, to not have them?

And the thought that strikes me the hardest—is there room for me in his life? In the family he's built with Lola and the larger circle he shares with Anna and her husband and children?

On Sunday, he's coming to my parents' house for dinner. He's going to meet Missy and Brennan. Yet he couldn't be bothered to invite me to dinner with his family tomorrow night. Or even tell me about it.

Or that he volunteers on weekends. It's like he has an entire life I know nothing about. A routine I'm set apart from.

My chest aches at the realization that I want this more than he does. That my feelings for him are stronger than his are for me.

That once again, I've set myself up for disappointment and hurt. For a broken relationship that won't materialize into the happily-ever-after I long for.

TWENTY

AXEL

ME: ARE YOU OKAY?

I HATE that Maisy took off after the game. Lola told me her stomach felt off, but it's strange that she hasn't messaged me. Or answered my phone calls.

I sigh as I slide out of my truck. Losing to the Hawks was fucking brutal. Not because I didn't see it coming but because I took some hard hits and couldn't get ahead of my opponents no matter how hard I tried. With my woman and daughter looking on, I tried really fucking hard.

Exhaustion weighs down my limbs as I walk toward my front door.

"Cheer up, buttercup," a voice calls out.

My head snaps up and I freeze. "You gotta be fucking kidding me."

Asher grins and stands from the top step of my porch. "Can't be all that bad, big brother. I'm here." He opens his arms wide, and I barrel toward him, catching him in a hard hug. Ash laughs and smacks my back while I pound his with my fist.

"What the hell are you doing here?" I pull back and

clasp his shoulder. His face is tan, his eyes blazing, his smile easy. Just like I remember. "I haven't seen you since—"

"My trip to Vietnam."

"Yeah, that was over a year ago. What are you doing here?"

Ash shrugs. "Didn't want to miss family weekend."

The fact that he would fly into town for Lola's weekend causes gratitude to rush my system. Raising a baby girl as a single dad wasn't easy, but for most of the hard parts, and the majority of the good moments, Asher always had my back. "Thank you."

His grin widens. "Come on. I know I'm flaky, but when have I ever not shown up?"

"Never." I unlock the front door and push it open. "How long are you here for?"

"Just till Monday. Then I'm heading to Charleston. I'm catching a fishing charter boat headed toward Panama at the end of the week."

"I can't keep up with you," I grumble, taking his bag from his shoulder and tossing it on the floor.

My brother chuckles, his eyes scanning my home. "You gotta nice place."

"Thanks."

"It could use a woman's touch."

I ignore his comment and head into the kitchen. Pulling two Coronas from the fridge, I pop the caps and drop two limes inside. Passing one to Asher, we cross the necks of the bottles before taking long pulls.

"What happened with Maisy?" he asks gently.

"Nothing."

"Come on, man. I'm your brother."

I shake my head. "Honestly, until about two hours, everything was fucking great."

"And two hours ago…"

I shrug, taking another sip of my beer. "I don't know. I'm meeting her family on Sunday. She sat in the family box at the game tonight. With Lola."

Asher leans his shoulder into mine. "That's big. And Lol likes her."

"I know. But after the game, I couldn't find her. Lola told me Maisy bounced. Something about a stomach bug."

"So?" Asher lifts his eyebrow. "Maybe she didn't feel well."

I shake my head, scraping my palm over my beard. "Nah. I mean, maybe not. But it's more than that. She's dodging my phone calls, not responding to my texts." I guzzle another gulp of beer. "Something's off. I can feel it."

I meet Asher's amused expression. The longer he stares at me, the more serious he becomes. "You really think so?"

I nod.

"Damn. If it was any other guy, I'd say you're kicking up drama. But not you, Axe. You hold everyone at arm's length until you let them in. Then, you care too much, get in too deep. You have any idea what could have spurred her to leave?"

I shake my head, confused and worried. Upset and annoyed. "Not a clue."

Asher shrugs and tosses an arm around my shoulder. "Free advice?"

"As if I'd ever pay you for it."

He laughs. "Let it lie tonight. Kick it with your brother and get a good night's sleep. Then, tomorrow, figure out where the hell you messed up and make it right with Maisy. She's good for you, man. I haven't heard you so happy in years and Lola agrees."

"You talked to Lola about me?"

He gives me a look. "Of course. There's literally no one else in your life who enjoys gossiping about you except me and Lol."

I snort. "Tell me about Patagonia."

We relocate to the living room and Asher launches into details about his trip. I listen to his wild tales, half in envy, mostly in awe. We laugh and joke, catching up on a year of conversation and bonding.

When I retire for the night, I'm grateful for Asher's surprise visit. Being with my brother always centers me, infuses my daily grind with a lightness I lack. But tonight, his arrival gave me a gift. A distraction from Maisy and the uncertainty about where we stand.

――――

ME: *You feeling better?*

I frown as I wait for Maisy to respond. I still haven't heard from her and, if it wasn't for Devon telling me that Mila met Maisy for breakfast this morning, I'd be concerned about her well-being. Now, I'm fucking concerned about our relationship.

Last night, I could almost believe that she didn't feel well and fell asleep early. But today, I know something's wrong. I don't like it. It leaves me unsettled, jittery. I hate feeling like I've lost control and right now, it feels like I'm about to lose my grip and spin out.

"Dad!"

I look up. "Huh?"

Lola rolls her eyes. "Where are you today?"

"Sorry," I mutter, shaking my head. "What'd you say?"

"We're meeting Mom, Ben, and the boys at the restaurant. Are you almost ready?"

I glance down at my jeans and black T-shirt. "Yeah."

Lola gives me an almost sympathetic look. Then, she walks into my room and reappears, holding out a blue polo. "At least wear a collar."

"Yeah, Axel. At least wear a collar," my brother repeats. Asher appears in the doorway looking suave and put together in a button-down shirt and dark jeans. It's a complete turnaround from the surfer boy look he rocked last night.

That's my brother, a true chameleon. He can have tea with royalty, conversing on international relations, as easily as working on a coffee plantation in Guatemala, slinging jokes in Spanish.

Lola grins. "I'm so glad you're here, Uncle Ash. Thanks for coming."

"Always, kid," Asher replies.

Sighing, I change my shirt.

Lola smiles. "Great." She glances at her watch. "We better get going."

Asher and I follow her outside to my truck. I check my phone one last time. Nothing from Maisy. I sigh, my worry morphing into unease, as I slide behind the steering wheel.

During the drive to the restaurant, Lola fills me in on her week, on an awful date Jas went on—she met the guy on Jdate but she's not Jewish so as far as her date's view on her being "misleading," I'd have to agree with him—and on her midterm exams.

Asher shares a story about a woman he met hiking and the incredible night they spent together when an unexpected rainstorm forced them to take shelter in the middle of a rainforest.

"What happened? Did you keep in touch?" Jas leans forward from the back seat.

Asher shrugs. "Nah, didn't get her last name."

"Uncle Asher! Are you serious?" Jasmine continues to lecture him, but I tune them out.

My heart's not in it because I'm caught up on Maisy. Did something happen at the game? Is she having second thoughts about me meeting her family on Sunday? Will I see her tomorrow?

"You should have invited her," Lola muses, breaking into my thoughts.

"What?" I glance at her in the rearview mirror.

"Maisy," Lola says. "I was surprised she wasn't coming to dinner tonight."

Next to me, Asher groans.

"Huh?"

Lola rolls her eyes. "She said you didn't mention it. But really, Dad?" Eyebrow raise. "Mom would have been happy to add one more to the reservation."

"Right." I slide my palm over the steering wheel. "Isn't it too soon?"

Asher shakes his head, reaching out to smack the back of mine.

"Ouch!" I duck.

"What?" Lola looks confused.

"Isn't it too soon for me to introduce Maisy to everyone?"

"She knows the team."

"Yeah, but that's work. This is...family weekend."

Lola narrows her eyes. "For my college. It's totally a casual vibe."

"And she invited you to meet her family," my brother adds.

"Right," I say again, wondering if I messed this up. Should I have asked Maisy to come today?

"You're meeting them on Sunday, aren't you?" Lola asks, falling back in her seat and banging her head against the headrest. "Dad," her tone is disappointed.

I work a swallow, connecting the dots. "Yeah." I merge onto the highway.

"So, you should have invited Maisy to dinner. Mom and Ben would love to meet her," Lola says.

"So would I," Asher points out.

"Next time," I mutter, my thoughts all over the place.

Is that what happened? Is Maisy upset that I didn't invite her? Should I have invited her? I never bring women around my family and, well, Asher, Anna, Ben, and their sons are my family. The only ones I have left since my parents passed.

Of course, I know they'd be thrilled for me if I met a woman to share my life with. Are Maisy and I there yet? She's still moving on from Josh, settling into her new job, and...introducing me to her family.

Fuck. I messed this up big time.

My phone chirps in the center console. Asher gives me a look, but I shake my head. The last thing I want is for Asher to read my text message to me. Especially if it's from Maisy, fibbing about how she's fine when she's clearly put out with me.

I should have invited her to dinner. I should have asked her to join family weekend with us. I should have and yet, I didn't.

"You should take Maisy fishing," Lola comments, interrupting my thoughts.

"Fishing?" I ask.

"You haven't taken her yet?" Asher gives me a look. "Do you need me to move here?"

I slug him in the shoulder.

"Fishing," Lola confirms. "That thing you like to do on weekends. You know, fresh air, peaceful, could maybe be romantic if you pack a picnic and don't hound her with fish facts the whole time."

"Hm," I grunt. "Fishing."

Lola sighs. Asher swears. I stew in the mess I've created, in the knowledge that I've let Maisy down.

My first date with Maisy, the one at Le Papillon where I wanted to knock Cohen's smile off his face, flits through my mind. We had talked about fishing.

Have I not included Maisy in my life enough? We sleep at each other's houses a handful of nights each week. I see her at work and take her on dates. We talk and share meals. The sex is off the fucking charts.

But am I missing a crucial piece to this puzzle? Am I letting her down without realizing it? Is she growing tired of my inability to commit the way she wants me to?

That's what sent Marisol packing. And it wasn't a year later that she walked down the aisle into the arms of another man. Anger beads in my veins, furiously zipping through my body, at the thought of losing Maisy to someone else. Of sending her into the arms of a man who isn't me.

Last night, I looked up and saw her cradling Scotch's son Fox in her arms and I felt like I got punched in the throat. I could see the longing in her expression. She held Fox like he's a treasure and, he is, but more than that, a treasure she wants for herself.

I glance in the mirror at Lola. Beautiful, smart, and grown at twenty-one years old.

Could I have another kid? Could I grow another family, the way Anna has with Ben? I glare out the windshield at the unassuming road ahead.

Do I want that? Does Maisy? Do we have a chance at creating that together?

"Dad, you're going to miss the exit." Lola points to the upcoming sign.

For once, Asher doesn't comment.

I flip on the turn signal and change lanes. Right now, I need to focus on dinner and be present for Lola's family weekend. Then, Maisy and I need to talk. Or clear the air. Or understand what the hell is going on between us.

———

MAISY: *I'm fine. Just crazy busy. I'll be at my parents' house early tomorrow so just come by around 5.*

I reread her message, complete with her parents' address, for the third time. Did she lie about not feeling well just to avoid me? What the hell would make her crazy busy between coming down with a stomach bug, seeing Mila for breakfast, and a handful of hours ago?

"You've barely eaten," Anna comments across from me.

When I look up, I meet the eyes of Lola's mother. Kind, unguarded, and concerned. I sigh. Anna and I kill it at co-parenting. Over the past two decades, we've become close friends and I consider her husband, Ben, to be one of my closest friends too. If I was going to confide in anyone about the wariness I feel about this thing brewing between Maisy and me, it'd be Asher and them. But...what the hell is even brewing between Maisy and me?

"What's going on?" Anna prods. She slips her son Damien a twenty-dollar bill. "I thought I saw an arcade next door."

Damien's eyes light up and he shoves his brother Adrian. "Dude, arcade?"

"Duh." Adrian stands from his chair. Shooting me a sly glance, he holds out a hand.

Chuckling, I slap a twenty in his palm.

"Ah, now you're spoiling them," Ben jokes, standing as well. "I'll go supervise." He kisses Anna's head. "Come on, Lol. I want to hear more about Jasmine's disaster of a date."

Lola gives me a curious look, but at her stepdad's prodding, she follows along.

Ben and Anna both give Asher a look, but he shrugs, sliding closer to the conversation by slipping into Lola's vacated chair. "I traveled a long way for the real gossip."

I snort.

Anna picks up her wine glass and takes a sip. We've been sitting around this table for over two hours, our family catching up, sharing silly stories, and joking around. We've celebrated Lola's success in her coding program, lifted a glass to Damien's scholarship prospects, and applauded Adrian landing the lead in his school play. Ben blushed as Anna filled me in on his new promotion and Ben's eyes gleamed with pride as he told Lola how Anna's hair salon was named Seattle's top salon this year. And, as usual, Asher had us all riveted with stories from the incredible adventures he's had over the past year.

Everyone was in sync and present. Everyone had great news to share. Technically, even me. But I've been distracted, my thoughts caught up on Maisy and the way she's avoiding me.

Did something happen? Or is it me? Has she come to her senses and realized I'm only a rebound? Does she not know how to tell me because we work for the Bolts? Or because she doesn't want to let me down?

"Axe?"

I look up, catch the worry in Anna's eyes.

I sigh gruffly and grip the back of my neck. Leaning back in my chair, I cross my arms over my chest. "I met someone."

Asher's hand lands on my shoulder, supportive.

In one heartbeat, Anna's concern dissipates and a hopeful joy flashes in her eyes. Still, her words are cautious, her tone hesitant. She knows how much I suck at talking, at discussing my feelings. Hell, it's one of the reasons why we didn't work out years before I blew it with Marisol. Carefully, she asks, "Who is she? How did you meet?" Her gaze shifts to Asher.

He dips his head. "I only know a smidge more than you."

"Hence, why you stayed instead of decimating my boys at pinball," Anna says.

Asher lifts his beer and takes a long drink, smacking his lips. "Exactly."

I glance at the ceiling, half of me dreading this conversation, half of me relieved I have my brother and another adult, a female, to get advice from. "Her name is Maisy. I met her over the summer. Her best friend is dating one of my teammates but now, she's working for the Bolts and..." And I blab out the whole fucking story like one of Lola's drunk sorority sisters seeking validation.

When I'm finished, Anna's rolling her lips together and I can tell she's fighting a smile.

Asher's less subtle. He chuckles loudly before polishing off his beer.

"What?" I give Anna a pointed look.

"I'm happy for you, Axel. You deserve this."

"Anna, I'm telling you she's avoiding me. She's barely responding to my messages and—"

"You hurt her feelings," she cuts me off, saying the

words like they're obvious. "You should have invited her today. You should have included her in meeting your family since she went out on a limb and invited you to meet hers."

"That." Asher points at Anna.

"Fuck," I mutter, hanging my head. "You know, when Lola mentioned it—"

"Lola figured it out before you?" Her smile is gentle.

"You got a smart kid," Asher tells me. "Be a proud parent for a second."

I glare back.

"It's time, Axel," Anna murmurs.

My glare turns toward her. Anna's smile grows.

"It's time to let someone in. It's been too many years and you've been on your own for too long. I know you don't have a lot of experience dating—" she holds up a hand when I open my mouth to defend myself. "And that's okay; that was your choice. But if you care about this woman, Maisy, enough to be twisted up over her, focused on what's wrong when you're out for Lola, then she means something to you. That's telling, Axel. That matters. Don't lose her."

"I agree," Asher chimes in.

I roll my eyes. "Why are you still here?"

My brother grins, looking between Anna and me. "It's like old times, isn't it?"

Anna laughs. "Axel and I having serious conversations and you just—"

"Providing the comic relief? Exactly," Asher fills in.

Anna shakes her head, amused.

"So, what do I do?" I redirect the conversation.

"Talk to her. You need to communicate. Have you let her in? Truly, let her in?" Anna asks.

I clear my throat, shaking my head once.

"Why?" Anna's voice is gentle, like she's talking to a

scared child. The way she used to comfort Lola when she was a little kid and had a bad dream or an argument with a friend.

"I don't want to be her rebound."

"And that was a perfectly acceptable excuse before you started caring for her. Now, it's just an excuse. If you were her rebound, she wouldn't bring you to her parents' house for Sunday dinner."

"I didn't want to overthink it," I toss out.

Anna laughs. "When have you not overthought anything, Axel?"

"True story," Asher adds.

I frown. "I don't know if I can give her the life she wants."

Asher heaves out a sigh and gestures to the server that he'll take another beer.

"What life does she want?" Anna leans back and crosses her arms over her chest, mirroring me.

I roll my eyes. "A husband, kids."

Anna nods. "You've talked about starting a family?"

"Not exactly," I say sullenly.

"Then, how do you—"

"She's a twenty-eight-year-old woman with a heart of gold. She's the kind of woman who should be a mother because she's always giving, always thinking about others. Caring."

"I can't wait to meet her," Asher says, his tone serious.

"And she wants to be a mother?" Anna lifts a perfectly shaped eyebrow.

"Yes. She's told me she wants kids. Then, I saw her, last night, at the game. She was in the family box, with Lola."

Anna smiles, leaning closer as if to encourage me to keep talking. I do.

"She was holding my coach's kid. A baby boy. And her face... Anna, if you could have seen her expression."

Understanding sweeps Anna's expression. "You don't want to let her down."

"I'd rather let you wax my back again."

Asher snorts and then, we all start laughing.

"That was a disaster," Anna mutters, recalling the incident in which I attempted this awful form of torture. "Ben and I still laugh about it."

"I tell it as an icebreaker on my travels," Asher admits.

I snort, swiping his fresh beer and taking the first sip.

"I'm letting you have that because you need it," my brother grumbles.

"Thanks," I mutter. "I don't want to break her heart. I don't want to let Lola down," I tack on.

"Lola?" Asher asks.

"Lola?" Anna looks surprised. "Axel, Lola is a woman. She's going to graduate college and forge her own path in the world. You are an amazing father, one of the best I've ever known. Your commitment to Lola and to the family unit we somehow managed to pull off is admirable. But you can't follow Lola around for the rest of your life."

"Can't follow me around either," Asher laments.

Anna continues, "Not even for the rest of your career. You've gotta let her go out and live for herself. And you need to live your life for you. Trust me when I tell you, Lola doesn't want you to do that alone. None of us do."

Silence fills the space between us as I process Anna's words. "Lola said that?"

Anna dips her head. "She worries about you. She worries what will happen if she gets a job offer or meets a man or goes off and decides to travel...she doesn't know what you'd do."

I close my eyes, feeling like a failure even though Anna just built up my parenting skills. "That's a lot of pressure on a young adult."

"It is."

"I don't want her to feel that way."

"Of course not. It's hard, letting them grow up and become their own people, isn't it?"

"This shit wasn't in the manual."

Anna laughs. "None of it was." Her eyes move to the window, to the arcade. "But we did all right."

"You guys did more than all right," Asher says, being serious.

"Yeah," I agree, taking a swig of my Coke. "What if it doesn't work out? With Maisy?"

"If you want it to, it will." Asher takes back his beer.

Anna tilts her head. "If it doesn't work out, then you move on and put yourself out there again. You're not the kind of man who is supposed to live his whole life following around the dreams of his daughter and occasionally casting a fishing pole."

I chuckle. "Yeah? Who am I then?"

"A man that gives. Just like the woman you described. Talk to her, Axel. Give her your best."

"Which is better than what you've been giving her," Asher adds, wanting to have the last word.

For being a good brother and showing up, I let him have it.

TWENTY-ONE
MAISY

"DID you see it in the light?" Missy shrieks, splaying the fingers of her left hand wide in the sunlight. The natural light causes the simple, beautiful, shiny diamond on her ring finger to sparkle like an endless promise. Like a forever.

"It's beautiful, Missy." The words scrape against the boulder clogging my throat. Not because I'm not happy for my sister. I'm elated. Missy deserves every happiness and I'm delighted she found that with a genuine man like Brennan.

But did it have to happen this weekend? Do I need to introduce Axel, a man who doesn't care if I meet his family, to my mom when she's flitting around announcing wedding plans like it's her upcoming nuptials?

Will she compare him to Brennan? Will she ask if he plans to marry? Will she have a coronary when she learns he has a twenty-one-year-old daughter?

Or will she bore us all, save for Missy, to tears with talk of cake tiers and color palettes?

I swallow back my bitterness. Missy's wedding is exciting and as maid—maid, not matron—of honor, it's my duty to care about flower choices and seating arrangements. And I do.

"Mais? You got a message." Missy points to my cell phone on the edge of the dining table in my parents' house. It's already cluttered with *Bride* magazines, venue options, and, wait for it, my parents' wedding album from the nineties.

I pick up the phone and the boulder in my throat expands.

Axel: We need to talk.

Words no woman ever wants to hear. Or read. Shit, is he ending this between us? Is he bailing on dinner tomorrow? Hope flares in my chest as disappointment knots my stomach. Do I want him to?

"There you are!" Mom enters the room, her gaze pinned on me. "I wasn't sure where you went."

I narrow my eyes. I've been here since this morning. I only popped out to get the bride-to-be the chai latte she desperately needed in her celebratory state.

Fuck, I'm jealous.

Guilt eats up my conflicting feelings of hope and disappointment until the only thing I feel is a clawing remorse for being a shitty sister. It's not Missy's fault that she caught Brennan's eye. Or that she's five years younger than me. Or that she made better choices with her romantic and professional lives and never allowed men to belittle her.

"We should start with dresses!" Mom claps her hand.

"But we need to know the color palette before we choose bridesmaid dresses," my sister points out, tearing her eyes away from her ring to sit at the table.

Mom sits beside her. "Well, let's start with yours." Mom gives me a sympathetic look as I plop down across from them. "You'll try to lose a bit of weight before the wedding, won't you?"

Missy stiffens, keeping her eyes trained on the magazine in front of her.

I work a thick swallow. It's not Missy's fault she's skinny either.

"Of course," I grind out, my insecurities over my body, over my choices, over my fucking life expanding.

"I think Maisy looks amazing," Missy comes to my defense. She offers me a smile. "You'll look beautiful in any dress and in any color."

"Except yellow," Mom says, opening a magazine. "Washes you out," she adds off-handedly, like a reminder.

"Here are my girls," Dad announces, entering the dining room. His hands land on the tops of my shoulders, squeezing some strength back into them. Dad's always the peacemaker, anticipating tension and trying to diffuse it before it can build. I've inherited my aversion to conflict and confrontation from him, giving my mother a green light to use her tongue like a whip. He kisses the top of my head. "Should I order some dinner?"

"That'd be great, Dad. I'm starving." Missy shoots him a grateful smile.

"Yes, we can have some salads or—"

I cut Mom off. "I'll take a burger."

"Same!" Missy nods enthusiastically.

"Burgers and fries it is," Dad decides.

Mom's mouth pinches but she doesn't voice an objection.

"We're having lemon chicken, mashed potatoes, and a kale salad for Sunday dinner," Mom says.

"Sounds good," Missy replies, keeping the peace.

"Is your friend still planning to come?" Mom asks. By

her tone, I know she doesn't mean anything by it. She's just confirming the final number of guests since Brennan's parents are coming. "Oh, and is Brennan's sister joining us?" She turns to Missy.

Missy nods. Mom's gaze returns to me.

Her question was completely innocent and yet, humiliation burns through me.

Is he coming? Are we still a thing?

Will I ever have a shiny ring on my finger?

I clear my throat. "Yep."

Missy's smile widens. Mom's does too. They're both happy for me.

And I'm...miserable?

"Excellent." Mom pats the top of a magazine. "Let's get to work before dinner arrives."

"Ooh, Mom, look at this veil." Missy nudges her magazine closer to Mom, her voice breathless.

Under the table, my fingernails cut into my palms as my hands clench.

Will I ever be worthy of a happily-ever-after? Of the stability and commitment of a partnership? Of the future I've dreamed of since I was a little girl playing bride?

Or will I really move to Costa Rica and spend my days surfing, alone?

My throat tightens and the backs of my eyes burn.

My phone beeps and I glance at the screen.

Axel: Are you home? Can I stop by your place?

I look at Mom and Missy, at their bent heads and excited smiles. I don't want to ruin today. I don't want to mess up Sunday. I don't want to detract from Missy's excitement, or hear Mom's comments, or spend another Sunday dinner aching on the inside as the only single woman at the table.

Me: At my parents. Let's talk tomorrow, after dinner?
Axel: OK

OK. I don't know how to read that. But right now, it doesn't matter. I have to get through this weekend and save the tiny shred of pride I have left. Even if it kills me.

"YOU OKAY?" Mila asks.

I close my eyes and lay back against the decorative pillows on my bed. I'm exhausted. So emotionally drained that I don't even want to toss my decorative pillows to the floor and pull back my duvet.

"I'm fine."

"Maisy."

"I'm happy for her. You know I am."

"Of course, you're happy for Missy. And Brennan," Mila says soothingly, her tone matching her words. "That doesn't mean you can't feel disappointment that your own life isn't where you thought it would be."

"It makes me a shitty sister. And an awful maid of honor."

"It makes you human. And when the people we love achieve milestones that we envision for ourselves, it makes our lack of them glaringly obvious. Why do you think I spent almost all the holidays at your parents' house after mine passed?"

I sigh, recalling that first Christmas after Mila's parents died. She was still dating Avery and he had an away football game. With his family traveling to the game and Mila distraught at the idea of being away from her hometown, her parents' burial sites, she spent the day with my family, oscillating between gulping wine and silently sobbing. Still, she didn't begrudge me for having parents who still uphold a slew of Missy's and my childhood traditions.

"I guess so," I say slowly. "It just cuts deeper because...I invited Axel to my parents' house for dinner on Sunday."

"And?"

"And he didn't invite me to meet his family—Lola's mom and her husband and kids—to kick off family weekend."

"Ah, I see."

"See what?"

"You're questioning everything with Axel."

"Wouldn't you?" I shoot back.

"Yes." She sounds miserable. True friend. "And you have been from the start."

Closing my eyes, I realize she's right. Everything with Axel feels like one step forward, two steps back. "I don't want to feel insecure anymore. I hate not knowing where I stand."

"I know."

"When we're together and it's good, it's amazing. The best I've ever had. But when it's not, I feel..."

"What?"

"Worthless."

"Shit," Mila swears.

"It's unsettling."

"Can you talk to him?"

"I feel like we're having the same conversation we had a few months ago."

Mila sighs heavily. "I don't think he's playing head games or doing this on purpose."

"I don't either," I agree. "Doesn't make it suck any less. Doesn't make me feel any better."

"No," my friend agrees sadly.

"I just have to get through dinner on Sunday. If my mom knows Axel and I are done beforehand..." I trail off, groaning.

"Introducing your man to your family isn't supposed to be a chore, Maisy."

"Trust me, I know that. But you know my mom. There're so many expectations involved and—"

"And you're an adult who doesn't need your mom's, or anyone else's, approval. I know Marge sucks at showing it, but deep down, she wants you to be happy."

"I know." Because deep down, I know my mom's intentions are good. She goes about things the wrong way. I've always been my dad's daughter and Missy's always been my mom's girl. Mom and I have never seen eye to eye but on some level, she'd hate that I felt this distraught at being honest with her.

"Talk to him, Maisy. Before dinner. Now. Don't let yourself feel all twisted up for one more day."

"I'm exhausted, Mil."

"Okay. I'm hanging up now so you can call Axel. You'll both sleep much better if you talk tonight."

I snort. "Night, Mila."

She sighs, knowing I'm not going to call him. "Good night, Mais."

I hang up the phone and clench it in my hand.

Before I can talk myself out of it, I send Axel a text.

Me: Hey. Can you talk?

I wait for ten minutes before giving up on a reply. With a dull headache and a heavy heart, I close my eyes and wait for sleep.

TWENTY-TWO
AXEL

MAISY: *Hey. Can you talk?*

I wince when I read Maisy's text. The time stamp says she sent it last night, when I was already passed out. Groaning, I pull myself from bed and head to The Honeycomb for an early skate.

Tomorrow, I'm meeting her family. When she first asked me, I agreed because I thought I'd be ready. I thought we'd be ready. Now, it feels like Maisy and I aren't in the position to take this next step. Not when we're barely speaking and any words we exchange are through a goddamn text. Not when it's all my fucking fault.

I should have invited her yesterday. I could have avoided this entire mess if I had a shred of foresight. If I didn't spend all my time overthinking everything and leaned into the moment, into the spontaneous and exciting unknown. If I lived even a bit of my life like Maisy.

"Fuck," I mutter, pulling my practice bag from the car and ambling toward the arena.

The locker room is quiet. Between the early time, the

fact that it's a Saturday morning, and the hangovers a few of the guys are nursing, I'm relieved no one talks to me.

I'm the first on the ice, taking the extra time to clear my head. The cool air washes over my skin, tempering some of the frustration heating my blood. I'm pissed at myself, worried about Maisy, and confused as hell. What the hell am I doing?

Why can't I get this right?

I fly down the rink, maneuvering a puck with ease, my head all over the place.

Coach Merrick blows a whistle and calls the team in. Coach Scotch runs through a few key points of this morning's practice and then, we break into smaller groups, working on specific skills.

"You okay?" the Rookie asks.

Fuck, he's a good kid. The kind of man I hope Lola brings home one day. "Yeah, I'm good," I lie. I'm far from good.

Today, it feels like every failure I've ever had, every mistake I've ever made, is stacked up in a nice, neat, long row of shortcomings.

Why didn't I heed Lola's advice? Or Anna and Asher's input? Why didn't I talk to Maisy before things got this out of control and now, she's barely speaking to me? I told her to never be scared to come to me and talk. I knew that communication was going to be the hardest, but most important element, of our relationship.

I fucking hurt her.

"Yo!" River flips his chin at me. "You here or not?"

I clear my throat, zeroing in on the puck that just shot past me. "I'm here."

"Wake the fuck up," River mutters.

Wrong day to start with me, kid. I growl, pushing off in

his direction. My one hand grips my stick and the other curls into a fist inside my glove. I'm ready for a brawl. I fucking itch for something I can release all my pent-up anger, shortcomings, and failures on.

"Whoa." Devon grips my arm. "Take it easy, man."

Turner gets in front of River and moves him away from me.

"What's going on?" Devon asks.

"Nothing," I spit out.

Devon sighs. "Get your head where it belongs. On practice. Then, call Maisy. Sooner rather than later."

He repeats the same warning from the other day but now, it sounds too late. To me, it confirms that I'm too fucking late.

———

AFTER A DAY SPENT on the UT campus with my family, I'm in a better headspace. I woke up early, took a hot shower, ate a massive breakfast, and had a fucking pep talk from Asher of all people.

Today, I'm ready to meet Maisy's family. I'm ready to show up for her, to have the hard conversation I've been avoiding, to go all in. I want her to know that I'm hesitant because this is new to me. Because I don't want to scare her off. Because talking about the future is a lot for me to process.

But that it's on me. None of it has to do with her. She's perfect and mesmerizing and fucking incredible. She deserves to know that my silence, my overanalyzing, my inability to make her feel like she's important to me, are my own shortcomings.

I need to own that and be upfront and say the words I've been holding back.

Dressed in a white button-down shirt and black jeans, I stand on her parents' front porch. I ring the bell and shift awkwardly, my nerves sky-high. I glance at the bouquet of flowers I purchased for her mom and grip the bottle of wine I brought along tighter. I hope this is appropriate; I hope I picked a good bottle. I hope—

The door swings open and a man in his fifties, with greying hair and a warm smile, says, "You must be Axel."

I return the smile, my cheeks tight. "And you must be Mr. Stratford. It's good to meet you."

"Same. Please, call me Judd." He holds the door open wider. "Come on in. The girls are in the kitchen. It's been a whirlwind of excitement this weekend." He gives me a look and a hearty chuckle.

My smile is frozen in place as I try to understand the meaning behind his words. Is the whirlwind because Maisy is bringing me home? Or did something else happen? Is this what Maisy was hinting at? When I thought she was avoiding me, was she really bogged down in family stuff?

"Missy and Brennan's engagement," Judd explains, correctly reading my confusion. "My wife is over the moon about it. Wedding planning..." He mock grimaces. "And as maid of honor, Maisy's been dragged into all the festivities. In my day, you were allowed to spend some time enjoying the engagement before everything else unfolded, but today," he sighs, placing a hand on my shoulder and walking us through the foyer and into the living room, "today, everything happens at warp speed."

"I know what you mean," I mutter, understanding father-to-father, exactly what he's talking about. "My daughter is twenty-one. It seems like she just started university and already, we're discussing internship opportunities and her resume, mortgage rates, and a 401K."

"Your daughter?" Judd looks surprised and I bite my tongue.

Shit. Maisy didn't tell her parents I'm a dad? Does it matter? Should it matter?

A slick mixture of pride and shame coat my stomach. Judd isn't looking at me with judgement, just surprise, and a hint of worry. Not that I can blame him. Maisy is a grown woman but she's still his daughter.

I know, from firsthand experience, that being understanding to another man's situation extends only as far as it affects my kid. Then, all bets are off.

"Yes, sir." My tone is gruff.

Judd sighs, his hand on my shoulder tightening. "You must have been young."

"Sixteen," I confirm.

"Must have been hard." His gaze lands on the framed photos of his daughters on the mantle. "I can tell you I had a hard time of it, and I was well into my twenties. Anyway, can I get you a drink? I'll tell Maisy you're here. Marge will want to touch up her lipstick before she meets you." He winks.

"A Coke would be great, if you have it," I say gratefully. "These are for your wife." I hold out the flowers. "And you." I hand him the wine.

"Too thoughtful." He smiles and I'm relieved when it reaches his eyes.

As Mr. Stratford steps into the kitchen, I move closer to the mantle. The photos are all of Maisy and her sister, Missy. They have a resemblance, the same golden hair and bright blue eyes. But Maisy's smile exudes warmth and an infectious energy, even through a photograph.

"Axel," her voice sounds behind me.

I turn and all the knots in my stomach, the tightness in my limbs, the worry and nerves and anxiousness I've been carrying around, unravels. She's standing in the doorway, a glass of Coke and ice in her hand, looking at me like she's both surprised and relieved to see me in her parents' living room.

I close the space between us. "Maisy, I—"

"It's so great to meet you, Axel!" Her sister cuts in, wrapping an arm around Maisy's waist.

My eyes plead with Maisy's. With the words I'm desperate for her to hear. *I miss you. I'm sorry. I want this to work. I want to talk.*

But politeness dictates that I turn my attention to Missy and hold out a hand. "Good to meet you, Missy. I hear congratulations are in order."

Missy squeals and holds up her left hand, flashing her engagement ring and doing a little dance.

In my peripheral vision, I note the way Maisy's mouth pinches, the slight slump in her shoulders as they round forward.

"It's beautiful," I force out the words.

"Brennan just proposed on Friday night!" Missy squeals, explaining how Brennan dropped to one knee in a field of wildflowers where they had their first date, a picnic, two summers ago.

Maisy won't look at me, and with each passing minute, I'm more aware of the heaviness in the air. I feel Maisy's discomfort as if it was my own and keep trying to catch her eye. I want, no need, that connection between us, but every time she meets my eyes, she glances away quickly. Too quickly for me to get a read on her, on this situation I've stepped into.

"Sounds like a dream proposal," I manage to say.

"It was," Missy agrees, squeezing her sister closer. "I'm so glad Maisy and you are here today. Brennan's parents are also coming for dinner and"—she leans closer, lowering her voice—"it's different now that we're engaged, you know?"

I nod, even though I have no idea what she's talking about.

"Mom is all about the wedding planning and it's helpful to have some other people, buffers, in case the conversation gets too intense," Missy clues me in.

I nod again. But fuck. What minefield did I just enter?

I look at Maisy, seeking guidance on how to navigate this, but her expression is flat. Her eyes placid. Like she doesn't know, or care, either way, how today unfolds.

I work another swallow. "Maisy, can we—"

The doorbell rings, cutting me off.

"Ah! They're here." Missy claps her hands.

A flutter of activity occurs that is so frenzied, yet well-orchestrated, that I step back and watch in awe. Mrs. Stratford flits into the room, swiping lipstick across her lower lip before capping the tube and slipping it into the pocket of her apron. She's untying the strings as her eyes scan the space, narrowing slightly on a throw pillow that, upon closer inspection, is tilted on the couch.

"Maisy, fix the pillow," she says, her gaze narrowing on her eldest daughter. "You didn't change? Oh, you know yellow washes you out."

Maisy fixes the pillow, her shoulders slumping further.

I frown, stepping closer to Mrs. Stratford.

"Oh! You must be Axel." She flashes me a charming smile. She takes my hand and gives it a squeeze. "I'm so glad you could join us today. Thank you, thank you so much for the beautiful flowers. I'm sorry it's such a rush today. With all the news!" She beams at Missy.

In the background, I hear Judd's voice as he greets the newcomers.

"Please, excuse me," Mrs. Stratford says, moving toward the foyer. Missy is already one step ahead of her.

I look at Maisy. "Is today a bad time?"

She looks at me, her eyes flashing with an emotion I can't read. Then, she laughs.

The sound is disjointed and emotional, an edge of hysteria I've never heard her emit.

"Maisy?" I frown, moving to her side.

She shakes her head, tucking her hair behind her ears and straightening her posture. She gives me a sympathetic glance, her eyes shadowed in apology. "Let's get through dinner," she mutters as her laughter dies.

Get through dinner?

My stomach sours and deep down, I know.

I'm too fucking late.

TWENTY-THREE
MAISY

I CRUNCH on another bite of kale salad, my head all over the place.

Beside me, Axel keeps shooting wayward glances. His brow is pinched, his lips thin, his worry obvious. Or is it discomfort?

I'm sure as fuck uncomfortable sitting around this dining table, nodding enthusiastically about the correct shade of white necessary for linen napkins at a wedding.

Unfortunately, Brennan's mom has a more rustic vision in mind and is pushing hard for the gingham checkered pattern.

But I digress.

"So, Axel," Dad says, trying like hell to shift the conversation away from wedding planning.

Mom and Mrs. Cutter speak louder. Missy's neck swivels between the two of them like a ping-pong ball, Brennan looks mortified, his father is half asleep, and somewhere, far, far away, I'm sure his sister is high-fiving herself for ditching this shindig altogether.

"She's in a computer science program. Coding," Axel responds to whatever Dad asked and shit, I wince.

I never told my parents about Lola. I never told my parents much of anything because I was going to fill them in on Axel this weekend, before today's dinner. Before Missy's engagement became the only plausible topic of discussion.

Silence descends on the table and Axel sits up straighter in his chair.

"You have a daughter?" Mom asks, her eyebrows raised.

"Yes, m'am." Axel wipes his mouth with a napkin. "Lola. She's a junior at UT."

"Maisy went to college there!" Missy exclaims.

"They have an excellent computer science program," Dad tacks on.

"And your ex-wife," Mom fishes for information, "does she live nearby too?"

I wish I could sink through the bottom of my chair, land in a puddle on the floor, and dissolve into air. Mortification blasts through me, heating my cheeks and making my stomach ache.

"Never married," Axel replies hesitantly.

Mrs. Cutter gasps, Mr. Cutter opens his eyes, and Brennan shoots me an apologetic look.

"Oh, well..." Mom trails off, her eyes darting to the Cutters. "More chicken?" she asks the table.

"No, thank you. It's delicious though," Axel replies, too polite for the treatment he just received.

"Have you kids thought about an organist for church?" Mrs. Cutter leans over the table, sparing a quick glance at Axel. "You must marry in the church before thinking about a family."

Dad rolls his eyes.

Sighing, I place my napkin down. Enough is enough. I thought I could get through this, but there's no way I'll sit here and allow Axel to be belittled, made to feel uncomfortable, in my parents' home. "Excuse us."

Standing, I tug on Axel's shirt. He gives me a surprised look, ducking his head and mumbling an apology. But he stands and follows me out of the dining room.

My pace is brisk, fueled by the anger burning through my blood. I don't stop until I'm through the front door, standing on the porch and glaring at the kids who ride by on bicycles.

"Hey," Axel says softly, closing the door behind him. He sits on the top step and I plop down beside him, mortified and miserable. "You okay?"

I snort. "Are you?"

His frown deepens, his eyes wary as they search mine. "I'm okay."

I roll my eyes. "Well, that's great for you." I know I'm being childish but...how is he not upset by Mrs. Cutter's remarks? How is he not bothered by the awkwardness between us?

How is he not devastated by the events of this entire weekend?

I sigh, trying to get my emotions under control. "You wanted to talk?"

"Yes."

I lift my eyebrows at him, waiting for him to continue.

He glances back at the door. "We don't have to do this right now. We can go back inside and—"

"No," I cut him off, shaking my head. I can't stand to have this awkwardness between us for another second. Besides, what are we going to sit down and pleasantly have a slice of pie before breaking up? Why else would he want to talk? My throat tightens and my nose feels itchy. I take another deep breath. "This isn't working."

Beside me, Axel jerks as if I tased him. "I know."

I close my eyes, hating the defeat in his tone. I want him to tell me I'm wrong. I want him to tell me we can fix it. I want him to give me something more than a calm, quiet agreement.

"When I'm with you, I feel like the best version of myself," I admit, turning to watch his facial expressions. "I love the way you see me."

Confusion flares in his eyes.

"But it feels like I'm more invested in this relationship, or whatever we're doing, than you are. I want you to meet my parents and you don't even tell me you're having a family dinner. I try to include you in my weekend plans. You never told me that you volunteer at the Children's Hospital. It feels like I'm pushing for more and I've already done that. With Josh, with my other exes. Even at my old job, with Tim. I'm tired of not being enough."

Axel's face darkens, anger eating away his confusion. His mouth twists.

But I hold up my hand before he cuts me off. "I want to be on equal footing. I want to have a *partner*, someone who doesn't make me feel like a burden, the way Josh did. Or an afterthought, the way you are. I really like you, Axel. A lot. But I'm done settling and this weekend, that's what it felt like."

"Maisy..." His voice breaks, his eyes pleading with me to understand.

I stare at him, waiting for his words. Waiting for him to say something that refutes everything I just unloaded.

"I care about you," he says finally.

"I know," I agree. I know he does. I know he's not playing mind games or intentionally trying to hurt me. "I care about you too. But I need more. Honesty and communication and to feel like I'm included in your life. To feel like we have some type of a future together. I'm not asking you to put a ring on my finger"—I wince at the bitterness that underlines my tone—"or promise me the world. But I want to get married one day and have a family and build a life with someone. You don't even want me to meet your family."

"That's not true."

"Then why didn't you invite me to dinner on Friday night? Or even tell me about it?"

Axel sighs heavily, raking a hand over his beard. "We've only been dating a few months."

I nod. He's right. It's only been a few months and yet, my shoulders drop and I lower my gaze to the ground. "It feels so much longer to me. I don't want to get hurt again, Axel. Any more than I am right now. And that's not on you; it's me. But I can't accept less than what I give, and it feels like I'm investing a lot more into this." I look back up, gesturing between us.

Pain rips across his expression, his eyes blazing. He opens his mouth and his phone rings. Axel swears, answering quickly. "What's wrong?"

Hurt expands in my chest that he would take a phone call in the middle of this conversation, but at the concern in his tone, I bite back my cutting remark.

Axel grips his messy manbun. "Yeah, man. There's a spare key in one of those fake-looking rocks. It's the third rock on the left next to that planter Lola made." He pauses. "No problem. I'll see you soon." He hangs up and his gaze swings back to mine. "Sorry." At the confusion in my eyes

—who is staying with him?—he adds, "My brother's in town."

It shouldn't affect me, but his words hit like the recoil of a gun. "Your brother's in town?" I repeat his words, my tone curt.

"Shit," Axel swears, closing his eyes. His innocuous statement just proved everything I said. I *am* an afterthought in his life. He's not letting me in, trusting me, the same way I am with him. A desperateness flares in his eyes as he stares at me. Seconds that feel like decades pass slowly. I give him time; I give him space to decide what happens next.

When resignation ripples over his expression, I fight for an inhale and drop my head. He doesn't fight for a different outcome. After a long pause, he warbles out, "If this is what you want..."

I swallow, my throat squeezing painfully. "It is."

Axel stands and reaches down for my hand to pull me up. His kindness, especially right now, makes my chest ache. "I'm not going to stop caring about you," he swears it, like a promise.

God, why couldn't we make this work? Axel is an amazing man. I know he is. He'd make an incredible partner. Husband. I already know he's the best dad.

I look down, unable to voice any thoughts.

He swears softly but his lips brush, featherlight, over my forehead. "I already miss you, Maisy."

Then, he moves down the porch steps to his truck. And I feel my heart crack in two.

———

"DID you give him a chance to explain things?" Mila asks.

I stuff another chip with guac into my mouth and nod.

"And?" she presses.

"He didn't say much. He kind of just agreed with me."

"Really?" She wrinkles her nose. "But Devon said—"

"What?" I bark.

Mila gives me a sympathetic look. "Devon says Axel is really twisted up over you."

Emotion floods my limbs. Preemptively, I swipe underneath my eyes, hoping to keep my tears at bay. "I don't think Axel purposely tried to hurt me, Mila. I know he cares about me. I know the things he felt, *feels*, for me are real. But I can't keep feeling uncertain about where I stand in my relationships. And yeah, maybe that's partially my issue. But Axel knew that about me.

"When I invited him to my parents' for dinner, he didn't reciprocate with an invitation to his family dinner. He never told me on Saturdays that he's going to volunteer at the hospital, just that he had stuff to do. Hell, he never mentioned that he volunteers anywhere at all! His brother's in town and guess what? I had no idea. He's never spoken of a future that doesn't hinge on Lola's plans. With how much I feel for him, in another year, I'd be devastated if there wasn't a future for us. It's better now, before I'm in even deeper."

Mila wraps an arm around my shoulder and tugs me into her side. "No one knew about his volunteering. I think it's something he's done for so long, it's just part of his normal routine. He told Devon that talking about it undermines the purpose of doing it. He doesn't do it for anyone except the kids."

I curl my feet beneath me and lean on my best friend. That's such an Axel response—such a good man response—

tears well in my eyes. In silence, we watch Lux swim around her fishbowl.

"He might just need more time." Mila's voice is low. "You're a game changer for him, babe. Not everyone sees their future as clearly as you do."

"He'd destroy me," I whisper. I already feel destroyed.

"Does this have anything to do with Missy's engagement?"

I shake my head. "I don't need a ring on my finger as much as I need to know we have a future. That we have *something*. Axel is always vague and cryptic. Not just his words, but his actions, too. That means something, doesn't it?"

Mila sighs. "I don't know. I hate seeing you like this, Mais."

"Axel was right about one thing."

"What's that?"

"He said we should take it slow. And I really thought I could but...my feelings for him are a giant rush. Maybe I need to step back and process. Maybe I need some time to get my own shit together before I try to involve someone else in my life."

"Or maybe you need to trust in what you and Axel were building and give him some time."

I snort, shaking my head. "You're supposed to be on my side."

"I am. I want to see you happy."

I pull back and look at Mila. "Do you think I made a mistake?"

She shrugs. "Not necessarily. It's just, it's weird to break up with someone when you both care about each other so much. There's something between y'all and the promise of more still exists."

"Then, I need him to show me that."

The corner of Mila's mouth curls. "True. Let's see if Brawler steps up and proves himself."

Sighing, I lean back against the couch cushion. "I'm not holding my breath," I say, but secretly, I hope Axel proves me wrong.

I hope he fights for us.

TWENTY-FOUR

AXEL

CHICAGO'S CENTER barrels into me, but I don't feel the hit.

My body is numb, my mind shutdown. I'm back to breathing pure hockey. Quickly, I gain control of the puck and flip it to Devon, watching as he flies down the ice. A sharp pass to Patton and we score.

Around me, the Bolts fans cheer, standing and clapping wildly.

I don't absorb their excitement either. I don't absorb anything except the heartbreak in Maisy's eyes when she admitted I make her feel like an afterthought.

A goddamn afterthought.

Disgust swells in my throat. I hurt her. Even though I think of her constantly, she never knew the depth. And why? Because I never told her.

Communication. The key element.

I fucked it up with Anna. I screwed it up with Marisol. And now, with Maisy. When will I learn? How the hell have I not grown emotionally since I was a high school punk with a baby?

"Yo!" Patton shoves me. "You good?"

"Yeah." I get back in position, my gaze zeroing in on the puck.

For the next four minutes, the game consumes me. Chicago is tough competition and even though we're down, we're not getting our asses handed to us. Under the leadership of our coaching staff, the team is starting to gel. We're getting into a groove and as Devon scores again, team morale spikes.

I manage a grin and a slap to Devon's helmet. It feels good, to play solid hockey with a great group of men, again. But it doesn't feel as good as it should because I fucking hurt Maisy.

"Get your head in the game." Barnes jerks his chin at me.

I acquiesce and check Chicago's center hard on the next play. He rushes me, gripping my jersey, and I grin. *Finally.* I let him at me for a handful of seconds, waiting for him to take the first swing.

Then, I lunge at him, relishing the adrenaline that rushes my system. Whipping off my face shield, I pummel the guy with a cross to his left cheek.

"You fucker," he growls.

I laugh, shaking off my gloves. He's giving me exactly what I want. "Thank you," I mutter before he's on me.

We brawl for a few minutes. In the background, I hear the sharp whistles, grunts from my teammates, some swear words. But I only have eyes for number thirty-four, and I relish beating on him. My anger, frustration, uncertainty, it all floats away as I unload on the dick who was stupid enough to start shit with me. Tonight, of all nights.

Eventually, the refs and the team break it up. The

Rookie and Devon pull me off the guy. He spits a wad of blood and I grin.

"What the fuck got into you?" Devon shakes my arm.

I shrug him off, falling back into old patterns. Re-embracing my nickname. I'm not called Brawler for nothing. "Just here to play hockey," I flip one of his bullshit lines from over the summer back at him and he glowers.

Dropping his voice, he hisses, "I know you're twisted up over Maisy but—"

"Don't." I glare at him, my expression hard. "Don't fucking go there."

He swears. "Get your head in the goddamn game, Brawler. That's an order."

I flip my chin in agreement, knowing that as Captain, he's trying to regain control.

But I don't give a fuck. Because I am here to play good hockey. And right now, I'm back to feeling nothing. Only numb.

———

MAISY: *Are you okay?*

She texts me an hour after I arrive home from the game. I pull a bag of frozen peas from the fridge and head to the couch. Leaning back, I drop the peas on my cheek.

Holding my phone over my face, I read Maisy's message again, as if it would have changed in the last five seconds.

It's the first contact I've had with her in four days, and it stings, even more than my face.

Me: Are you?

Maisy: No. How's your face?

Me: No worse than everything else.

Maisy: I'm sorry, Axe.

Her words gut me, and I wince. She shouldn't apologize for me making her feel unwanted. Unworthy. Not enough.

Her apology makes me feel fucking worse.

Me: You have no idea how sorry I am, Mais. Get some sleep.

Maisy: Good night.

Dropping my phone next to me, I close my eyes. I wish I was better with words. I wish I could tell Maisy just how much I want her, care for her, can see a future with her. I just don't have all the details sorted yet. I know I want her by my side, but I don't know if we'll marry, or have kids, or live in Costa Rica.

Can I give her all of that? Can I make her happy enough to stay with me?

A loud knock on my door ruins my peace. It's gotta be Lola and Jasmine.

"It's open," I holler.

The door swings open. "Figures," a male voice says.

My neck whips around since Asher left on Monday—with a stern warning to get my shit together—and there aren't any other males who would waltz into my house. I swear as Devon, Rookie, Barnes, Turner, and River fucking Patton filter into my kitchen.

"What are you guys doing here?" I resume my position and lay the peas on my cheek.

"Helping you get your head out of your ass," Barnes says cheerfully.

"That was some fight, mate," Turner offers as he plops down on a chair in my living room.

"You knocked him around pretty good," Patton confirms, a begrudging kind of respect underlining his words.

"All of that cause Maisy Stratford's got you tied in

knots," Devon states, going where none of the other guys would.

I glower at him through one eye.

He smirks and sits down on the other end of the couch. "What's your plan?"

"Huh?" I ask.

"To win her back," he says, spelling it out for me. He's pushing the same way Anna did with her gentle words and kind eyes. The same way Asher tried with his snarky remarks and smacks to the back of my head.

I close my eye. "She's done with me."

Barnes snickers as Patton looks at me in disgust.

"What?" I ask Patton.

"Never took you for stupid," he mutters.

Turner bites back his smile.

"You gotta do something big," the Rookie muses. "Something special."

"Something no one else has done for her," Devon agrees.

"She doesn't want to be with me," I say, even though the words ring false. She does want to be with me, just not this uncommunicative, emotionally stunted version. And can I blame her? Hell fucking no. Because I'm the one who mucked everything up.

"Stupid," Patton hisses.

I throw the peas down and glare at my teammates. "She deserves better."

"Then how you're acting?" Patton lifts an eyebrow. "I agree."

"Do you want to be with Maisy or not?" the Rookie asks, cutting to the heart of the matter.

"More than anything." The words are out of my mouth before I can stop them. I duck my head, embarrassed.

But the Rookie smiles and Turner looks relieved.

"Something big," Devon reminds me. "Special."

"She doesn't care about material things," I shut them down. "I need to prove to her that I'm all in. That I want her as part of my life. That she's not just some *afterthought*." The word tastes like shit on my tongue. "But at the center of everything I want. Everything we're building. My whole goddamn future."

"There ya go." Patton nods.

Barnes claps. "Finally."

"Huh?" I ask again.

"You're getting your head out of your ass. We knew you could do it," Turner explains.

I heave out a sigh. It's almost a relief that I don't have to front with these guys. "I care about her."

"We know," the Rookie agrees.

"I'm falling in love with her," I admit, telling them the truth that no one, not even Maisy, knows.

"We know." Turner's voice is soft. Understanding. At the lack of judgement in his tone, it's clear he's the eldest of five.

"Something big." Damien leans back in his seat, crossing his arms over his chest.

"And special," I muse, before an idea explodes in my mind. Sitting up straight, I snap my fingers. "I got it." I laugh, surprising, or scaring, my teammates. "I fucking got it."

"What is it?" the Rookie asks curiously.

I shake my head. "Wait till I tell you this."

They all lean forward, as if we're in a huddle, and I tell them exactly how I'm going to win Maisy back.

Exactly how I'm going to show her she can trust me. That we have a future. That there will always be an us.

"YOU SURE YOU'RE OKAY?" Missy asks, pinching the stem of her champagne flute.

"I'm more than okay. I'm happy for you." I manage to smile, which relaxes her some.

I am happy for her. Seeing my baby sister try on wedding dresses brings tears to my eyes. As Mila pointed out, I can be happy for Missy while also being disappointed for myself. But I'm not showing that today.

Nope, today is all about Missy finding a dress style she adores. When she comes out of the dressing room clad in a strapless gown complete with a sweetheart neck and a big, princess skirt, my breath catches in my throat.

"You look perfect," I tell her.

She beams, twirling, as Mom claps her hands. "Put that one aside, Mis. You'll want to try it on again."

Missy admires herself for a moment in the floor-to-ceiling mirror as the sales ladies and two of Missy's friends gather around her.

Next to me, Mom sighs.

"What's wrong?" I ask.

"You're not happy."

I cringe at the callout, my mouth dropping open. "I'm not—"

"I didn't mean it as a criticism," Mom cuts me off. She gives me a long, searching look. "You and I always approached things differently, you know."

I nod at the truth in her statement. I'm a nonconfrontational people pleaser and Mom's an assertive perfectionist.

"And I know sometimes, I'm hard on you," she adds, taking a sip of her champagne. "But all I've ever wanted is for you to be truly happy. For you to see yourself the way other people do. The way I do."

"What?" I murmur, her words hitting me in my emotional feels. Tears gather in the corners of my eyes.

"Oh, Maisy." Mom reaches for my hand and squeezes. "Watching Missy try on dresses is making me sappy." She laughs before looking at me. "That man cares about you."

"Axel?"

Mom nods. "I knew it the second I met him. The past few months, you've seemed happier too. Brighter, as if you're glowing with life. I don't know what happened between y'all but I can tell you, as your mother, that it's worth diving into. Love is always worth diving into." She brushes a wayward strand of hair over my shoulder. "It was wrong of me to harp on you. I thought if you didn't look or act a certain way, you wouldn't land a good man. That's the way my mama raised me, and I guess I repeated that cycle with you. But Axel, well, he's certainly a man."

I snort, caught off guard by my mom's candor. I hope she continues.

"And he cares about you for exactly the woman you are. Bright, optimistic, with an overflowing heart." Mom wipes her eye as I choke up from her kind words. "Don't ever lose that, Mais. And dive back in."

"Mom! What about this one?" Missy calls out, appearing in a new dress.

Mom gives me a soft smile, stroking my cheek once, before turning to Missy and responding in her usual, no-nonsense tone. "I love the neckline."

I sit for a long moment, considering Mom's words. Reveling in the affection and honesty she showed me. It's not that I've never had heart-to-hearts with my mom before, it's that they're rare. They occur eons between frequent judgement and criticism. But I've never doubted that deep down, she loves me and wants me to succeed. To fall in love and be happy. *Dive back in.*

Can I? After everything I've been through with Tim and Josh, can I give Axel the benefit of the doubt? I don't doubt his intentions, but his actions, coupled with words, never felt solid enough. By cutting things off, am I ending it too soon? Am I denying us both a chance at true happiness by not taking the risk with him?

Mom leaves me with much to consider. The past week, since Axel and I quietly broke up, has been awful. I've spent nights crying myself to sleep, mornings pep-talking myself to drive to work, and afternoons nibbling on dough-nuts. I've lamented my poor taste in men to Mila who quickly pointed out that Axel doesn't fit the description.

He doesn't. He's incredible.

Somehow, knowing that makes it worse. I miss him. The scent of his cologne, the randomness of his text messages, seeing him at work. I miss listening to the gravelly pitch of his voice. I dream about the feel of his heavy hand stroking my back and the half-smile, still a mystery, he flashes my way.

I gulp my champagne, polishing it off and placing the flute on the table beside me.

Fuck. I'm in love with Axel Daire. I have been since the beginning. Deep down, I've known it since the wine and paint date.

By letting him go, it's like I've stabbed myself in the heart. Everything aches and seems hopeless without him, without the possibility of an us.

My pep talks fall flat. My manifesting doesn't inspire. My heart feels too heavy for my body and my head, too tired for life.

I've never felt like this before. Empty and emotionally depleted. Hurting from my core outward. It's as if my very essence has withered away.

Is this true heartache? Every breakup I've had in the past pales in comparison. Axel and I only shared a few months together and now, my life feels different, lacking, without him.

I wick a tear off my cheek.

I'm in love with Axel Daire and I turned him away.

By doing so, I broke us both.

———

"GO AWAY. IT'S SUNDAY," I remind Mila when she bounds into my bedroom the following morning.

"It's almost noon." Disappointment is heavy in her tone. I ignore it.

"I'm taking my key back."

She laughs.

"I'm emotionally hungover." I crack an eye open.

Mila wrinkles her nose. "When was the last time you showered?"

I close my eye.

"I came to give you a heads-up." She plops down on the end of my bed.

"For what?"

"Seeing your sad state, I'm relieved I came by."

"Mila," I warn, wanting to know what the hell is going on.

"Axel will be dropping by your house in an hour."

"What?" I jackknife straight up in my bed.

Mila grins evilly. "If you don't want to look like a hungover—"

"It's emotional," I remind her.

"Hot mess, then get your ass in the shower." She points to my bathroom.

"Why is he coming?"

My best friend runs an imaginary zipper over her lips and tosses me the key. The same way she did in high school.

"You're the worst," I huff, but excitement blooms in my chest and I force myself out of bed.

"I'm the fucking best," she refutes. "Otherwise, I would have let him see you like this." She gestures to my frame, clad in an oversize UT hoodie and cheetah-print boy shorts.

I laugh, the sound surprising me because...how long has it been since I laughed. Okay, dramatic much?

"Go shower!" Mila yells, pointing at the bathroom door again. "And I'll try to pick out some casually chic outfits for you."

"Thank you! You're the best. I mean it!" I call over my shoulder, hurrying to the bathroom.

The second the hot water hits, I spring into action. Axel is coming here. Why? He must want to talk.

Does he want to get back together? Does he think we

can salvage our relationship? Does he think we have a chance at a future?

Now that I've acknowledged to myself that I love him, *am in love with him*, his visit feels like the most significant moment of my life.

Whatever he says will determine my future.

And I know, deep down, that I want to build one with him.

TWENTY-SIX
AXEL

MY BREATH CATCHES when she opens her front door.

She looks good. Beautiful. So much better than I feel.

Has this past week not been torture for her? For me, it's felt like someone shoving bamboo sticks underneath my fingernails, even after I had a plan. Even after I knew I wanted to win her back.

"Hey," I mutter, glancing down at my shoes.

"Hi." Her tone is light. "I'm happy you're here."

My eyes snap back to hers. "You are?"

She nods, opening the door wider. "Come on in."

I cross the threshold and my shoulders relax as relief flows through me. I missed her house. I missed her space. Fuck, I missed me with her.

I follow her into the kitchen. She turns and leans one hip against the countertop, her eyes on mine. "Coffee?"

"Okay." I sit on a barstool.

Her goldfish swims around in the fishbowl, unaware of the tension, of the heaviness, unfolding in the space.

"Thanks." I wrap my hand around the mug when she places it down in front of me.

"Sure." She leans back, taking a sip of her coffee.

After a beat of silence, I realize it's now or never. I need to be all in, invested and talking about the future and the vision I want for our relationship, or I need to leave this kitchen and let Maisy Stratford go so she can move on and build a life with someone else. Like Anna. And Marisol.

Ha. As if I'd fucking let that happen.

Sighing, I grip the back of my neck and tell her the fucking truth. "I'm in love with you, Mais."

Her mouth drops open.

"I'm fucking crazy with want for you," I continue. "I don't know how to say, never mind explain, all the things I feel for you. But it's intense. It messes with my head. It makes me question pretty much every fucking thing."

"Axe."

I shake my head. "Let me get this out."

She nods.

"I'm sorry I hurt you. I'm sorry I couldn't give you more, more of what you needed, from the jump. And I'm sorry as fuck for not introducing you to my family when I should have. I hate the impression I left when I met yours."

"You didn't—"

"I wanna man up, Maisy," I say before she can stop me. "I wanna man up and be your man. The guy you count on. The one you know always has your back, is in your corner, and you can say whatever the hell you want or feel however you wanna feel and know, with certainty, that I'm not going anywhere. That I'm yours. And you're mine."

She gasps at the possessive edge in my tone, but I don't care. I want all of her. And I want everyone to know it.

I pull an envelope out of my back pocket and slap it on the counter between us. "Give me another chance. A real chance to show you, to prove to you, that you're everything I want in a partner. That the future you dream up is the one I want to live, with you by my side. Give me time, please, to be worthy of every damn thing you selflessly give to me."

Hesitantly, she reaches for the envelope. Pulling out the paper inside, she gasps. "Witch's Rock."

"I want to take you to surf camp," I say, snorting at the end. Asher knew exactly what camp Maisy had mentioned and helped me plan the trip. How fucking ridiculous will I look on a surfboard? And who fucking cares. "I want to hang in Costa Rica with you and do yoga on the damn beach. I want to live out your dreams, with you, because you're *my* dream. I was just too scared, too clueless and closed off, to admit it."

"You're, I, for real for real?" Her eyes are wide, searching my face as if I'm going to prank her.

God, she's the best woman I know. "For real for real," I confirm. "I'm not ready to hang up my skates yet. And I gotta wait for Lol to graduate. But then, Costa Rica, Europe, hell, even a small fishing village in Maine, I'm in for whatever you want. And I'll build us a house, you'll make it a home, and we'll fill it with kids. Whatever your heart desires, I want to give you. I just need a chance to prove it."

Tears well in her eyes, tracking down her cheeks. I'm off my stool in an instant, rounding the kitchen island, reaching for her. "Don't cry."

"They're happy tears," she sobs, wrapping her arms around me. She sinks into my arms and cries against my chest. "I swear, I really am happy."

I hold her close, breathe in the scent of her hair. "I missed you too fucking much."

She pulls back and looks up at me, her blue eyes dark with unshed tears. "I love you, Axel. I love you so much that if this doesn't work out, it will destroy me."

"Never." I push her hair away from her face and cup her cheeks. "There's not a chance this won't work between us. Because one week without you was the worst week of my life."

Her face crumples again and I pull her closer, kiss her forehead.

"For me too," she admits, wiping her fingers underneath her eyes. "I was miserable."

"I never want you to be anything but happy."

"We're really going to surf camp?"

I chuckle. "Asher sent me a Hawaiian shirt and board shorts."

Maisy laughs and hugs me again. I grasp the back of her hair and tug lightly, until she lifts her face to mine.

"I know it's too early, but I'm done waiting. I never wanted to be your rebound—"

"My what?" She laughs, like the thought is inconceivable.

I shake my head. "Be my home, Maisy."

Her eyes hold mine, serious and earnest. "Always."

Then, I press my mouth against hers and kiss her hard to seal the deal.

Maisy Stratford is mine. She's my greatest weakness. And my greatest fucking strength.

TWENTY-SEVEN
MAISY

AFTER HOT COFFEE and a heartfelt conversation, my heart is bursting. But my body, well, my body is a greedy little bitch.

I tug on Axel's hand and even though it's only two in the afternoon, I lead him to my bedroom. When we cross the threshold, his eyes widen as he drinks in the mess of my usually immaculate space.

"I kinda gave up on life this week," I admit, clearing piles of clothes from my bed.

He snorts. "And I thought I was the only one nursing a broken heart."

"Not even close." I spin around to face him. My hands settle on his arms, slide up to his shoulders, and meet behind his neck. "I felt lost without you."

Axel's hand settles in the small of my back, his palm flat, his fingers splayed. It's as if he wants to touch as much of me as he can. "Let's find it again."

"What?"

"Me and you," he replies, his lips brushing over mine.

I lift my face to his and arch into his chest. He deepens

the kiss, dragging my body up his frame and slipping his tongue into my mouth.

Whimpering, I close my eyes and drop my head back, loving the onslaught of his kisses. Loving the way he devours me like he'll never get enough. I know I'll never have enough of him. Axel is all consuming. Powerful and intentional and larger than life.

My hands track his back as he hitches my body into his arms. My legs encircle his hips as his fingers dig into my ass.

"Missed this ass too," he mutters, making me laugh.

In the next breath, I'm laying down on my bed, spread out underneath him. He smirks. "Love looking at you like this." Then, Axel covers my body with his and gives just as much as he takes.

Our kissing turns greedy. His hands roam my skin with abandon, working me out of my clothes as quickly as I pull his off.

"Christ," he mutters, his eyes drinking in my naked breasts. His hands slide up my sides. "Love these fucking curves," he mutters, dropping his head to suck one pert nipple into his mouth. Before I can respond, his fingers delve between my thighs and, as needy as I am, my knees drop open and my hips tilt upward, egging him on.

Axel growls as he yanks my thong aside and presses against my clit. The sound alone is enough to make me come. It's hot and desperate and possessive as hell.

I shiver, digging my nails into his back as he lays over me, raining kisses along my neck, his fingers working magic between my thighs. I reach for him, groaning as my palm closes around his hard length.

"Fuck, you're wet," he says as the sounds of my arousal, the sounds of him spreading it over my clit and working his fingers in and out of my core, meet my ears.

"For you." I sound breathless.

"Better fucking be." He grows even harder, like steel, in my palm.

I pump him slowly, both of us torturing each other, until it's too damn much.

Axel pushes me back and hovers over me, lining up at my entrance. "You want me, gorgeous?"

"Badly."

A vein on his neck jumps. "Never as much as I want you." He pushes inside of me in one sharp thrust that has me crying out in pleasure.

Axel sets a furious pace, his hips thrusting, his fingers playing with my clit. I don't tear my eyes away from his, getting lost in the depths of midnight, drowning in his need, soaring in his want.

"I'm close," I pant, holding on to his forearm as he rocks into me.

"Come for me, Maisy," he demands, looking down to where our bodies repeatedly join. "Let me see you come."

I do. So fucking hard, I shake and quiver, crying out his name. Over and over as tremors of pure bliss wrack my body.

"Fuck." Axel follows a moment later, spilling himself inside of me, and collapsing on top. He rolls to his side, taking me with him and nestling me against his chest. "That was..." He breathes out, at a loss for words.

"I love you." I kiss his pec.

He laughs. One of those loud, boisterous, one-in-a-million laughs. "I fucking love you, Maisy Stratford."

I snuggle closer and his palm settles in the middle of my back, anchoring me to him. Right where I belong.

"And this is for real for real."

AXEL and I must doze off after our epic reunion sex because the next thing I know, it's dark outside and an incessant knocking is happening on my front door.

"Who is it?" Axel asks.

"I don't know," I reply, shifting in his arms.

"Mila?"

"No, she has a key." Which, she used earlier today to pull my ass from these rumpled sheets.

Grumbling, Axel moves from my bed and tugs on a pair of sweats. Immediately, I feel the loss of his heat, of him, from my bed.

"Stay here," he advises, moving toward the door. A moment later, I hear him swear. "What the fuck do you want?"

Panicked, I wrap myself in my sheet and stand from my bed, taking the whole damn sheet with me like a Bridgerton up to no good.

"I, uh, so, is Maisy home?" a male voice asks.

And it's a male voice I recognize. "Josh?" I blurt out when he comes into view.

Josh's eyes widen as he takes me in, sexed-up hair and a bedsheet.

Axel growls and Josh redirects his gaze. "I asked you a question," Axel reminds him.

"I, um"—Josh's eyes dart to me again—"I was hoping we could talk, Maisy."

I wrap the sheet tighter, tucking it under my arms. Axel narrows his eyes at me, clearly hating the part where Josh is seeing me in a bedsheet. "I have nothing to say to you."

Josh shuffles on the front porch. "Yeah, I just wanted to apologize."

Silence. Josh glances between Axel and me.

"Where's the fucking apology?" Axel spits out.

"Oh, right," Josh stammers, his eyes finding mine again. "I'm sorry, Maisy."

"Okay, thanks, Josh," I say, turning back toward my bedroom. I thought his apology would mean something, but it doesn't. One week without Axel showed me just how worthless my other relationships were. They didn't add anything to my life, or I wouldn't have been able to move on from them so quickly. Right now, Josh's presence is an annoying interruption.

"We could get back together!" Josh calls after me, deluded.

Axel laughs. I turn to glance at him, drinking in the view as he stands in the doorway, dusk behind him, and howls at the moon with laughter. "She's moved on."

Josh frowns, his eyebrows dipping together. He points at me, then at Axel. "You think this is going to last? Look at you, Maisy. You're not the right woman for—"

Axel growls, a warning and a threat.

I hold up my hand. "I'm not interested, Josh. You heard my boyfriend. I moved on. Take care of yourself."

"Boyfriend?" Josh sputters, incredulous.

"For now." Axel crosses his arms over his chest. "One day, she'll call me husband. Now get the fuck out of here and don't bother my woman again. Unless you have a real apology for the shit you pulled, don't even talk to her." With that, Axel slams the door and stalks toward me.

I frown. "Are you really mad?"

"Mad?" He shakes his head. Then, he picks me up and the sheet falls to the floor. I squeal. "Not mad." Axel moves back to my bed. "Just want to remind you that you made the right fucking choice." He pulls my duvet over our naked bodies and drops kisses down my stomach. When his mouth meets the sensitive space between my thighs, I drop my head back and laugh.

"It was never a choice. It was always you," I say.

Axel drags his tongue up my core and I gasp. "Not taking any chances," he says, before doing it again. "Not with you."

Then, he gets to work on making me orgasm. And I close my eyes and enjoy every second of it. For real for real.

EPILOGUE

NINE MONTHS LATER

Axel

I BREATHE in the salt water and sunshine and plant my surfboard in the sand. Narrowing my eyes, I scan the ocean for my woman, and I grin when I see her. She's clad in a sleek black wetsuit, but I know, underneath, she's rocking a sexy-as-fuck green bikini. Maisy catches a wave and I pause to take it in. Damn, seeing her on that surfboard, riding the waves as fearlessly as she rides my dick—okay, sorry, that was a bit much. But man, she is a goddess.

So much so, that I lay my board down and sit on it, wanting to watch Maisy in her element. To appreciate her determination and soak up her joy. She pumps her fist in the air when she reaches the shoreline. I pump mine back.

She blows me a kiss before rushing back into the sea, wanting to set up for her next wave. Maisy is a natural at surfing. Well, she's a natural at most things.

Much more so than I am. But that's okay. I like hanging back and watching her. I like just being along for the ride.

Since Maisy and I made things official, everything in my

life has improved. I learned to relax a little, to stop over-thinking and overanalyzing every decision. It's made me a better father, a better brother, a better teammate, and a better friend. All in all, Maisy has made me a better version of myself.

Isn't that beautiful? Isn't that the fucking point? If you're going to share your life with someone, shouldn't it be the person who pushes you to be more, to be the best, to grow into all you're capable of?

She topples off her surfboard and I straighten. A moment later, her face breaks the surface of the water, and she shoots me a sheepish look, laughing at herself.

I smile and settle back down.

I had an incredible season with the Bolts. The team is gelling, the guys have become like family, and the future looks promising. Lola's gearing up to start her senior year of college and is already fielding job offers from tech conglomerates and start-ups in Silicon Valley and Austin, Texas.

I love knowing that her hard work is paying off. That she has a sea of options and endless resources at her disposal. I love seeing the woman she's growing into, but more than that, I love that she now feels the freedom to explore her options.

After Lola graduates, I don't know where I'll end up. With Maisy, of course, but I'm not sure where. Maybe here? I glance around at the stretch of sand and sparkling sea.

Leaning back on the board, I drink it all in. The truth is, I don't care where I go if I'm doing it with Maisy. I think of the small ring box tucked into the side pocket of my suitcase. Tonight, I'm going to propose. I'm going to slide a delicate but beautiful two carat oval diamond ring on her finger. Tonight, I'm going to start the next chapter of our lives together by asking her to become my wife.

Tonight, it's happening, and I couldn't be more excited or hopeful for what's in store for us. As my future fiancée says, good things are on the horizon.

———

THANK you so much for reading *Brawler's Weakness*! I hope you loved Maisy and Axel's story!

CURIOUS ABOUT THE ROOKIE? Beau Turner's little sister is coming back to town... If a teammate's sister trope is your jam, don't miss *Rookie's Regret*, coming September 8!

ACKNOWLEDGMENTS

Thank you for all the love and support that went into Maisy and Axel's story!

Melissa Panio-Peterson, Amy Parsons, Erica Russikoff, Becca Mysoor, Dani Sanchez and the Wildfire Team, Virginia Carey, the wonderful women of Give Me Books Promotions, and Amber — all of my thanks and gratitude for your encouragement, advice, and support!

For the covers of this series, I had the great joy of working with Niagara-based photographer Stephanie Iannacchino (www.stecchinoo.com) and these fantastic athletes, and now, cover models: Justin, Manny, Evan, Brady, and Tony. Thank you for collaborating on this project with me!

A million thank you's to the bloggers, early reviewers, bookstagrammers, booktokkers, YouTubers, and romance readers everywhere for checking out my books and diving into this new series. I hope you're falling for the Bolts!

T, A, R, & L — all my love. Always.

ALSO BY GINA AZZI

Tennessee Thunderbolts

Hot Shot's Mistake

Brawler's Weakness

Rookie's Regret (September 8)

Playboy's Reward (November 3)

Hero's Risk (January 5, 2023)

Bad Boy's Downfall (March 2, 2023)

Boston Hawks Hockey:

The Sweet Talker

The Risk Taker

The Faker

The Rule Maker

The Defender

The Heart Chaser

The Trailblazer

The Hustler

The Score Keeper

Second Chance Chicago Series:

Broken Lies

Twisted Truths

Saving My Soul

Healing My Heart

The Kane Brothers Series:

Rescuing Broken (Jax's Story)

Recovering Beauty (Carter's Story)

Reclaiming Brave (Denver's Story)

My Christmas Wish

(A Kane Family Christmas

+ *One Last Chance* FREE prequel)

Finding Love in Scotland Series:

My Christmas Wish

(A Kane Family Christmas

+ *One Last Chance* FREE prequel)

One Last Chance (Daisy and Finn)

This Time Around (Aaron and Everly)

One Great Love

The College Pact Series:

The Last First Game (Lila's Story)

Kiss Me Goodnight in Rome (Mia's Story)

All the While (Maura's Story)

Me + You (Emma's Story)

Standalone

Corner of Ocean and Bay